the

LION'S

den

also by Eliza Freed

the
LION'S
den

ELIZA
FREED

Brunswick House
New York

Brunswick House Publishing
244 Madison Avenue
New York, NY 10016
First Brunswick House ebook and print on demand edition: January 2016
The Brunswick House name and logo are trademarks of Brunswick House
Publishing, LLC.
The publisher is not responsible for websites (or their content) that are not
owned by the publisher.

Manufactured in the United States of America
ISBN 978–1-943622–02–3 (ebook edition)
ISBN 978–1-943622–03–0 (print on demand edition)

For Charlie.
You'll never have to worry . . .
your brain and your soul are extraordinary.
I love you.

There were times when I felt completely alone.
Even when he was standing right next to me.
He would tell me that's ridiculous.
He would convince me I never felt it.

prologue

JAMES HAD SLEPT IN. HE must be getting sick—he never slept late. My son lingered in front of the open refrigerator door, staring inside, which was a habit that drove Brad crazy.

"Close the door," Brad said and ate another spoonful of cereal.

"Where's the milk?" James surveyed the counter and opened the refrigerator door again.

"What milk?" Brad asked never looking up from his phone.

"The milk for cereal," said James, and I looked at Brad's bowl.

"You used all the milk?" I asked, and Brad put his phone down. He was suddenly the center of attention.

"Yeah."

"What about the kids?"

"What about them? Make him some toast."

I shook my head and found the bread in the drawer. "I used to make him milk from my breast. I would never finish the milk before the kids have eaten." I tried to understand how he could have done it, and he was watching me as if I were crazy. Maybe I was crazy.

"I'm not going to argue with you over milk." When I walked by, he grabbed my elbow. "I'll argue with you about whatever you want, but not milk. We're better than that." Brad smiled and somehow swayed me. I softened at the glimpse into our old life.

"I made him milk from my breasts," I said dramatically, trying to hold back the laughter. "What have you done?" Brad laughed, too. "No, seriously, since your initial DNA donation, what have you done for these children? And do not say, 'I work.'"

"I picked you." Brad kissed my cheek, and my heart stopped for a moment. They were the first words of appreciation he'd said to me since I'd quit my job. The first glimmer of acknowledgement, and although it was a half-compliment half-joke to him, it meant the world to me.

LIV'S LEGS FLEW WELL OVER her head as she swung in the backyard. The swings were always my favorite, too. I'd wanted to fly. Her hair flew in front of her face as her legs pumped backward and then blew behind her as she soared forward.

"I love you, Mommy," she yelled toward the kitchen doorway I watched her from.

"Love you, too." I took a deep breath. I could pull this off. I could raise these children to flourish, I could be with Brad, and I could have Vince. It didn't matter where I lived, or that I only worked twenty hours a week at the police station. It would be more than enough.

"Watch me! I'm flying."

"I see you. You are flying."

Brad walked into the kitchen.

"You have to come see Liv. She's swinging so high the whole swing set is rocking."

He came and stood behind me, and we both watched our daughter as she soared through the sky. "She loves it," he said, sounding almost sad. It caught me off guard. I thought annoyed was Brad's only emotion.

"Hey, Brad?"

"Yes." The annoyance returned.

"What do you love about this town?"

The silence behind me followed his breath down my back. It left me chilled with the familiar longing of isolation in its wake. Even in Brad's presence, I felt alone. Or was it especially in Brad's presence?

"Funny you should ask." His tone had an edge of anger, as if he were pissed about something and waiting for the perfect time to fight about it. "I was thinking that maybe you're right. Maybe we should move."

I didn't even turn around. I wasn't going to ruin the moment of watching Liv swing with a discussion about moving. Brad loved it here. He'd made us move here years ago, and we weren't going anywhere.

But why would he bring it up now?

Brad moved closer and swept my hair to one side. He put his hands near my collarbone and ran them down to my shoulders, massaging them with a foreign touch. The slight edge to his tone rested at the end of his fingertips as he pressed his hands into my skin.

"Would that make you happy, Meredith?" He tightened his hands on my shoulders, kneading the muscles beneath his grip.

"You're kidding," I said, challenging him, not wanting to pay attention to this conversation. Liv leaned way back until her head nearly touched the ground and her feet almost reached the sky. Brad's hands moved up to my neck and tightened there.

"Just say the word."

My breath caught. My instincts kicked in, and I exhaled slowly, not letting Brad feel the difference. His hands still rested around my neck, and everything seemed to move in slow motion except Liv yelling to the sky that she was awesome as she soared through the air.

"I'll let you know," I said with a controlled lightness. I tapped his hands, stifling the fear with a fake jovial movement.

Brad let go and I stayed, watching Liv, feeling safe in her presence. She would protect me from whatever he knew.

Brad went to the bathroom, and I continued to stare out the doorway as the rotting sense of death rose up inside me. I swallowed hard to try to force it back down, but it was there and wouldn't be ignored.

I e-mailed the colonel. There was no subject and nothing in it.

one

Chief Vincent Pratt

I USUALLY DIDN'T CHECK FOR an e-mail while I was on duty. She was here with me most weekday mornings, but today was Sunday. She was home with her family, and I was working. There was no nine-to-five for police officers. Not even the chief.

So I looked. I knew there wouldn't be a new one, but when I missed her, I'd read the old e-mails, anything to feel closer to her, to have her tell me something. She wrote me every night before she fell asleep in her husband's bed.

Her bold-faced address at the top of my inbox shot adrenalin through me like electricity through a wire until I saw there was no subject. I leaned my arms on my desk with my phone in my hands, holding my breath as I opened it.

There was no content.

The silence in the station surrounded me until the air conditioner turned on and blew cold air over me from the vent above. The rule I never thought would come up, the one that I was sure we'd never need, had been invoked. I went back to my inbox, hoping for another e-mail explaining that she'd sent the first one by mistake, but Meredith Walsh never made mistakes. I was her only one.

The day she read her extensive list of rules to me, I'd thought she was paranoid, but I didn't care. I would follow her rules if she needed me to. No calling, no texting, and no using her name. She was the most thorough person I'd ever met. I'd laughed at her as she'd listed her demands one by one so seriously but without any clothes on. I wasn't allowed to fall in love with her, but even then, I knew I'd already broken that one. And this one: If I ever send you an e-mail with no subject line and nothing in it, you are to delete your account immediately and NOT contact me. I wanted to break now. The fact that she was married to another man was only tolerable because I could see her almost every day. This e-mail, this direction to stop contacting her, choked me with jealousy. Even though I knew it was to protect her children, not Brad Walsh, I still couldn't stop the anger at the helplessness welling up inside of me.

There'd been a few months she hadn't spoken to me. They'd been the worst of my life—worse than boot camp, the police academy, and Kuwait. Worse than anything, and now, it was going to begin again. I had no choice but to wait for word from her.

I scrolled down my inbox. For so long these e-mails had been the only piece of her I was allowed to have. For almost a year, I had only these words and two days a month to see her. They were our secret that taught me what it felt like to live, and now I couldn't bear to delete them. I stared at the screen. Every e-mail in the account was from Meredith. She was the only one with the address. No one else in the world knew it existed, just like our relationship.

I searched for the ones where she'd told me she loved me. It took forever for her to believe we *could* love each other and that love could be a component of an affair. But I'd loved her before I'd had an affair with her. I'd loved her the first time I'd met her.

I found the one she'd sent last Thursday morning before she'd come to work. I'd read it, and instead of working, I wanted to drive her somewhere, anywhere we could be alone. But what Meredith yearned for was to not have to be alone. The subject of the e-mail was "I always dream of you."

I had a dream last night we were out to dinner and everyone in town stopped by our table to say hi. You were wearing the Phillies T-shirt, which forced me to touch you the first time. Yes, I think it was the shirt that caused this. After dinner, we met John and Jenna for drinks.

We were real.

The frustration I'd felt when I'd first read the e-mail came flooding back. She insisted she'd never divorce her husband and that we'd never do things other couples did. It killed her that our relationship only existed in the dark, but Meredith had created the impossible situation.

I scrolled up to my reply.

We are real. We're just different. You are a huge part of my life. Whether the rest of the town knows it or not. I love you.

I searched through the list of e-mails I couldn't bear to lose and considered printing some out or forwarding them to my personal account, but Meredith would kill me. I found account preferences and selected Delete Account and All Data.

There was nothing left to do but wait for her. A forbidden text, a Facebook message, both of which I knew would never come. If she sent this e-mail, her husband knew something or suspected something. She wouldn't risk a shred of evidence of our relationship being found. I'd spend every minute looking for a sign until I heard from her. I'd check the windshield of my car for a handwritten note. I'd watch the door to the police station each time it opened, hoping she'd found an excuse to come in on her day off. I knew I'd drive by her house while out on patrol today, anything to catch a glimpse of her.

I wouldn't make it through the night without hearing from her. Not tonight. Not any night.

I PULLED THE POT OFF the burner and put my cup directly

in the flow of coffee. I couldn't wait for the archaic machine to finish brewing the whole pot. I hadn't spoken with Meredith, and I hadn't slept a minute last night. I'd driven by her house twice yesterday, but the house was empty. Even after dark, no lights were on. It was as if she'd disappeared.

She'll be here soon.

Swim practice started early. Her son's age group was at eight thirty. She'd be here. She was going to walk through the door, and I already had an excuse ready for why I needed to talk to her in my office with the door shut.

I replaced my mug with the coffee pot and tried to calm down. This was yet another rule we were going to break, because I wasn't ever going through a night like last night again. Daniels came in and grabbed a cup off the counter. One of the cups Meredith had bought for us.

"Hey, Chief. Did you hear about Meredith?"

My chest tightened, trapping the air inside of me, where it surrounded my heart like a vise. "No. Hear what?"

Daniels moved around like nothing was a big deal. Like Meredith hadn't sent a warning that her husband knew we were having an affair. "She fell at her house. I just saw Jack from the Rescue Squad at Wawa. He said they transported her yesterday. I was hoping she called out sick. That you heard something."

"No calls." I wasn't sure if I was speaking aloud. "Is she okay?"

"Unresponsive."

Without a word, I put my cup down and walked out of the station.

When I turned off Main Street, I switched on my siren and lights and sped to the hospital, breaking every rule. Not caring. It wasn't going to matter after I killed Brad Walsh.

two

Brad Walsh

LIV WAS SO TIRED SHE couldn't walk. None of us could. I told James he had to man up because I couldn't carry them both, but he looked like a little boy. My back throbbed as I tried to fit Liv in behind the driver's seat of my car that wasn't meant to transport children. I should have brought Meredith's.

Her name sent a pain from one side of my head to the other. Meredith.

How did this happen?

Sixteen hours, and she still hadn't woken up.

What if she never wakes up?

The kids had cried nonstop the first hour until I'd convinced them she'd be fine. But when she didn't wake up, I just wanted them to go to sleep, too. Their sad eyes churned the guilt like acid in my stomach. She had to wake up. She had to come back.

Both Liv and James were asleep before I exited the parking lot. I'd just turned off the radio and was pulling my phone from my pocket when a police car flew by with its lights on. Whoever was driving must have been going a hundred miles an hour. I watched in the rearview mirror as the car careened into the emergency entrance's parking lot.

Maybe a cop's been hurt.

I had my own problems to worry about. I glanced at the

kids in the back seat. The nurses had been good to us. By eight last night, the kids had started complaining they were hungry, and I just wanted them to shut up. I wanted their mother to wake up and shut them up. "Look around, take note of where we are," I'd snapped at them. I was a dick. Taking care of them was not my job. Meredith did that, but now she wouldn't wake the fuck up. If I didn't know better, I would have sworn it was just to spite me. But that was crazy. She might have hated me. Even enough to leave me one day, but she'd never hurt the kids.

One at a time, I carried my children to their rooms and placed them in their beds. I kissed their foreheads and told them I loved them. Meredith always tucked them in. But today was different. They were going to bed at eight A.M. instead of eight P.M., and I was the only one home. I needed to sleep myself. The exhaustion descended upon my body. Every step was an effort I could barely expend. The nagging feeling wouldn't go away, and I knew I wouldn't be able to sleep until I had some answers. Some answers as to how we ended up here, with Meredith unconscious in the hospital.

I walked through the house. The front door was still unlocked from the day before. Once the paramedics had taken Meredith, the kids and I closed the door and ran to the car to follow her. I locked it. I needed to be alone with her things. Her phone lay at the bottom of the steps next to the plant she fought so hard to keep alive. I bent over, grabbed the phone, and paused at the plant's hearty green leaves. It was finally thriving, and so was Meredith. It'd taken her years to accept her life here, and she was finally settling in.

The phone had flown past me when she'd hit her head. I'd wanted her to face me, but I'd also wanted the phone. I wanted to know what the hell was going on with my wife. Two months ago, I'd seen the strange text message to Jenna. But Jenna was her best friend, and they were always talking in some code.

Meredith: This is me. Saying the word.

Jenna: Nibac.

I told myself they were trivial.

I didn't understand a word of it. It meant nothing. But it had tormented me. Something changed with Meredith. A quiet peace had descended upon my house, upon my marriage, and I wasn't stupid enough to take credit for it.

I traced the lock pattern with my finger and opened her world captured in her phone. I started with the texts. The ones I'd seen to Jenna were missing, making me wonder for a second if I'd fabricated them. I went through every message. Practice times, playdates, birthday parties, babysitting, talent show . . . They were all about the kids. Jenna's were the only entertainment, and most of her texts were comments about the pain of motherhood. Many of the names I barely recognized. Our children's lives were Meredith's domain.

I exited the texts and proceeded to invade every app on her phone, starting with the photos. There were tons of them. Liv and James were in almost every single one. Some I recognized she'd sent to me when I was away on business and she knew the kids would want me to see whatever they were accomplishing at that moment. The photos were useless.

I read her e-mails. Every single one of them. There had to be over a thousand—teachers, volunteers, mothers, coaches, etc. Again, all of it pertained to our children. One group was about a lunch date with her friend, Christine, but that was a year ago. I kept going back. A few e-mails from college friends. All were innocent. Not one shred of evidence there was a part of Meredith's life I didn't know about. I listened to her voice-mails. Most were from me. I scrolled through the Instagram account she clearly never went on, and finally Facebook. I went right to the messages and found nothing. Nothing noteworthy at least. It was as if Meredith's entire existence stemmed from Liv and James. I looked through her profile and ran my finger across the pictures she'd been tagged in from Christine's wedding and Sarah's Christmas party. Both events I'd sent her to alone. She hadn't even shown me a picture when I'd returned. I wasn't a part of them.

It was crazy. The whole fucking thing was crazy. My heartbeat pounded in my head. It blocked out my thoughts and forced me to look at the staircase. The sight of the pooled blood sent the pounding to the back of my throat. I turned away, unable to face the evidence of her injury. My wife, the mother of my children's blood was on the stairs, and she was in the hospital. This couldn't be my life.

I abandoned her phone on the dining room table and walked into the kitchen. The refrigerator was filled with birthday party invitations and schedules for the kids' teams. There were pictures of Liv and James covering every other inch of the door.

I'd imagined the whole thing. I was going to go upstairs and sleep, and when I woke up, she was going to be here kissing James's forehead or laughing with Liv.

The humid wind blew outside, and I opened the kitchen door. The heat hit my face as I watched the swing blow toward the trees. I was standing in the exact same spot we'd stood in when I'd said the words to her. The words that had been eating away at me. The words I knew meant more than I'd ever let myself believe.

"Say the word," I said again, this time to no one.

The last time I'd said those words, her neck had been in my hands, and she'd been watching Liv swing. If I hadn't known every inch of her body as well as my own, I might have missed the catching of her breath. I'd fought against my hands tightening around her neck, and Meredith's breathing had returned to normal within a half second. She'd made some joke, but I wasn't listening. I hadn't heard a word she said. All I remember was the anger that crept up inside me. I'd had to leave the room and find some place I could process her reaction to a text I couldn't understand. A text that no matter how many times I told myself meant nothing, taunted me until I finally said it to her.

And even though it still made no sense, I couldn't let go of the idea that there was someone else. I grabbed her purse off the kitchen counter and rummaged through it. Frustrated with all the pockets inside, I turned it over. Band-Aids, ChapStick, the kids' favorite gum, and a random assortment of other things spilled onto the countertop. Even her purse was depressing. There was an empty Ziploc bag, and as soon as I opened the seal, I knew the bag had held a joint at one point. Based on the rest of her life, I no longer blamed her for smoking.

Nothing.

Not one thing came out of her purse that told me anything. But I knew. I knew she wouldn't be in the hospital if I hadn't said those words, and those words wouldn't have set the ugliness into motion if she weren't hiding something or someone from me. I pulled myself up the back staircase. I would search through her nightstand and her entire closet, but even before I began, I knew I wouldn't find anything. Meredith was smarter than I was, and she would never have an affair. She was better than that.

Better than me.

three

Chief Vincent Pratt

I SAW BRAD WALSH'S CAR. I almost turned around, but I had to see Meredith first. I pulled the cruiser into a spot right out front and grazed the hood with my hand as I walked toward the entrance of the emergency room. I was going to grab him by the shirt collar and bang his head against the hood of the car until he told me exactly what he'd done to her.

The image of her on top of that same hood fought past my rage at him. Meredith had texted me: This is me. Saying the word. It was the phrase that would finally end our separation, and I'd sent back: Nibac, telling her in code to meet me at the cabin. When she got there, I'd put her on top of the car and took back what was mine.

I closed my eyes right before walking into the ER, and in my mind, I could still see her that day. She'd been flustered and angry, and then she'd surrendered to me, confessing for the first time that she loved me.

"Chief Pratt, what can I help you with today?" The receptionist's voice reminded me I was in uniform. I was in the real world.

"Morning, Delores. I heard one of our employees was brought in yesterday, and I wanted to check on her." My voice was light. As if Meredith was not the center of my world. As if I hadn't spent the entire night twisted in knots of worry and fear because I hadn't spoken with her. "Meredith Walsh."

Recognition spread across Delores's face. It was a small town with a small hospital, but if Delores heard about a patient brought in yesterday, there was a story to tell. "She's in ICU. Go ahead up."

The questions raced through my mind, but I had to see her. I skipped the elevator and took the stairs two at a time, racing toward her and pulling one deep breath into my lungs before opening the door on the third floor.

"Hi, Chief," the first nurse who saw me said, as if this were just any Monday morning.

"I need to see Meredith Walsh."

Keep it light, colonel. I heard Meredith's voice in my head, calling me colonel so if she ever spoke in her sleep, no one would know it was me she was talking about.

"Oh, 'tranquility.' That's what everyone on the floor's calling her. She hasn't made a sound." I kept a straight face. "How do you know her?"

The muscles in my chest tightened, threatening to rob me of my fake, easy demeanor.

Why is she silent?

"She works at the police station."

"Oh. We had no idea. I would have called you." I moved toward the patient hallway, hoping the nurse would move too. "You can see her." She stood and stepped out of the nurses' station with me an inch behind her. "She hasn't woken up yet, though."

I dropped back a step and tried to regain some control over myself.

She hasn't woken up yet.

I turned the corner into her room door and relaxed at the sight of her. Meredith looked like herself. She was here. We were together. But when I walked farther into the room, I saw the ugly purple bruise on the other side of her face. It disappeared under the white bandage circling her head. The anger was choking me. I held on to the footboard of her bed and fought the urge to pick her up, carry her to my car, and take her away.

"What happened?" I asked to no one, but the nurse assumed it was to her.

"Her husband said she fell on the stairs and hit her head." The e-mail with no subject and no body flashed through my mind, and on the heels of that was the image of Brad's neck in my hands. "Wooden stairs. That's why I made my husband put carpet on all our stairs. For God's sake, look at her. It could have been a baseball bat that hit her."

I studied Meredith's marred face. The image burned itself into my mind, and she was never going home to her husband. The deal was off. "Who's her attending?"

"Dr. Evans."

"Where is he?" I stared at Meredith, willing her to wake up.

"I'll call him for you." The nurse's voice was low. I was scaring her, but she was moving faster than she was before. She left the room and left Meredith and me alone. I buried the need to lean down, kiss her, and whisper in her ear that I was here and I loved her. I knew it would only make her mad. She wouldn't want our relationship to come out like this. The last thing she'd done before whatever happened was protect our secret. She'd sent the e-mail.

Dr. Evans came within minutes. He shook my hand, and I hid the tension coursing below my skin. He reviewed her chart and read every word before addressing me. "She's beautiful, isn't she?" Was the first thing he said, and I wanted him to stay away from her, too.

"What's going on?"

"They brought her in yesterday. Unresponsive from a fall down a wooden staircase. No broken bones, but there's some swelling and it's causing pressure on her brain. We drained some fluid last night. We're just waiting for her to regain consciousness."

"Do you think she fell?" My fingers dug into the footboard until pain shot through my nailbeds.

"It's hard to say. It must have been a violent collision. I've never seen a fall this bad, but that doesn't mean it couldn't happen."

I pulled my card from my wallet and handed it to the doctor. "Call me as soon as she wakes up. Before you call anyone else."

"She's going to have one hell of a headache."

"Call me." I held his eyes for a moment too long, but I needed to be here before Brad Walsh.

four

Brad Walsh

EVEN FROM THE BACK OF Meredith's giant closet, I could hear the knocking. It was like a battering ram on the wooden front door.

Who the fuck?

Deciding it was probably just a nosy neighbor, I continued to shift through another section of jackets, checking the pockets as I went. Whoever it was, they didn't seem to take a hint, though, because they were still pounding on the door. It continued until I thought the door was going to collapse under the force of it, and I had no choice but to answer.

I was halfway down the stairs when I spotted the police cruiser in the driveway. *Great.* Meredith's new coworkers were now involved in this mess. I expected it to be one of the young officers, checking in since I hadn't called and she was supposed to be at work. When I opened the door, Chief Vincent Pratt was standing in front of me.

"Hi, Brad," he said pleasantly through a taut jaw.

"Hi, Chief. You here about Meredith?"

"I am. Do you mind if I come in?" He nodded toward the house as he asked but walked past me without waiting for a reply. I kept my eyes on him as I closed the front door. He scanned the living room, the dining room where Meredith's phone lay on the table, still agitating me, and finally, his scrutiny froze on the bloodstained staircase. We both stared at it. The guilt rose in the back of my throat, and I hated this dickhead for being here with me.

"Sorry I didn't call and let you know she wouldn't be in. It's been a long night." I was a victim here, too. *You've got this, Brad.* "I'm sure you understand."

The chief nodded. He was used to conversations like this. I was not. "What happened?" He turned toward the stairs again, his eyes fixed on where the blood pooled on the tenth step. It was the tenth out of thirteen. It ran down the side of the stairs and splattered against the wall behind them. A few drops had landed on the ninth stair. I counted them again. One, two, three . . . yes, the ninth stair. "Brad?"

"Sorry." I looked away from the grotesque scene. I ran my hand across the back of my neck and massaged the sore muscle near my shoulder. I needed to sleep. "I'm not really sure what happened," I lied.

"Well, just tell me the parts you are sure about."

"We were watching Liv swing out back. She was going so high, and Meredith insisted I come see her." He stared at me. I wanted him to look away. Look back at the bloody stairs, anywhere but at me. I started to sweat, which I didn't want him to see. "Do you want something to drink?"

"Sure." He waited for me to lead the way. I realized he'd never been here before. I walked into the kitchen with the chief behind me, opened the cabinet, and reached up for two tumblers. I pulled the water pitcher Meredith always kept full from the refrigerator and filled the glasses. When I turned around, he was touching her wallet, pushing it away from the rest of the contents of her purse. "Looking for something?" he asked.

I took my time and a sip of water. He couldn't rush me. Even if I did just want him to leave. "Her insurance card. Apparently, the hospital likes you better if you have insurance."

He nodded and kept poring over the items on the counter. "So you were watching your daughter swing. Then what happened?"

"I went upstairs. I heard a scream and a thud." The echo of her scream sent a shiver down my sweat-covered back. "I ran out and found her on the staircase. She scared the shit out of me." I took another sip of my water and watched the chief to see if he believed me. He was staring at me without a hint of kindness or understanding, so I added, "She still is . . . scaring me."

"Were you two having any problems? Any recent arguments?"

"No. It was an accident. A horrible accident. Everything was perfect between us."

Vincent Pratt didn't move. He didn't blink. He stood across the island from me, staring at me, and I wasn't backing down. She was my wife, and I was the one here when she'd been hurt. A harsh vibrating sound came from under the contents of Meredith's purse.

"What's that?" Pratt asked without taking his eyes off me. Rather than no emotion, his jaw was now tight and his lips were almost in a sneer. He hated me, but I was probably imagining that. I was tired and worn. And Meredith still hadn't woken up.

"It's my phone," I said and reached under the bag of Band-Aids from Meredith's purse. I pulled the phone out and saw it was Dharma calling from her desk phone, which I'd told her a hundred times not to do. *Fucking idiot.* As if I didn't have enough to deal with right now with this cop in my face.

"Aren't you going to answer it? It could be the hospital."

"No. It's work." This seemed to piss the chief off more than anything else.

I do work, after all.

I was losing my patience with him. "If you don't mind, I need to sleep before my children and I go back to the hospital."

He inspected every inch of me, and I still thought he wanted to kill me, but then his scowl broke into a kind smile, which was even more unsettling. "Of course. I'll let you get some rest. When you see Meredith, tell her everyone at the station is asking about her."

"I will." I followed the bastard to the front door. He peered into the dining room again at her phone and then up to the stairs.

I opened the door and the bright sunshine beckoned him out of my house of horrors.

Get the fuck out, dude.

five

Chief Vincent Pratt

IF IT WEREN'T FOR MEREDITH'S precious children sleeping in their beds after a night at the hospital with their mother, Brad Walsh would be dead. Meredith and I would become the *Dateline* episode she'd always predicted. If given the chance to convey what a complete asshole he was, I think a jury would let me off.

I called the station to check in. Really, it was just an excuse. I needed to use my phone and confirm it was still working. Why hadn't the hospital called me yet? Brad needed to go to sleep, and Meredith needed to wake up. She needed to tell me exactly what happened so I could see him in handcuffs in the back seat of my car. *God help him.*

Meredith was always honest with me, but there were subjects we rarely spoke about. Her husband and my wife were the main two. But even with only the few things she told me, I knew Brad and Meredith's marriage wasn't perfect. She'd been making love to me for almost a year, which kind of made perfect impossible.

Instead of speeding, I took my time. I rode with the windows down and let the heat fill the car. I needed to ground myself before I lost control, drove back to Meredith's house, and beat her husband's skull into the staircase that still had her blood all over it. She had to wake up soon.

I stopped the car, and the clicking of my turn signal increased my pulse. My mind fixated in on the rapid, repetitive sound until I was ready to kill someone. Brad Walsh. I steered the car onto Jenna and John's lane, and the clicking stopped. I took a deep breath. My phone rang with a call from the hospital. I slammed on the brakes and answered before it rang a second time.

"Chief Pratt?"

"Yes. Dr. Evans, is she awake?" I needed to calm down. I'd have the whole town talking, and that was the last thing Meredith wanted.

"She was." The doctor hesitated, and I threw the car in park and waited for what seemed like an hour for him to begin again. "Mrs. Walsh woke up. She was in a great deal of pain and agitated, so we sedated her for now. If you want to see her, try after dinner."

"Besides the pain, is she going to be okay?"

"I think she's going to be fine."

"Did she say anything about how her injury occurred?" I held my breath.

"She doesn't remember a thing. In fact, she seems to have lost her memory of several months before the accident." I held my breath as every memory I had of Meredith flew through my mind. Her naked and laughing on the couch in my hunting cabin. The way her eyes deepened in the dim light of a hotel room in Philadelphia. Her low but powerful voice as she first told me she loved me. Meredith forgetting was impossible.

"How?"

"Amnesia is common with head trauma. There's no definitive calculation for how far back the amnesia extends or how long it'll take to regain the memories. We'll know more when she wakes up again. We sent her down for another CT scan to make sure things are moving in the right direction."

"Thanks for calling," I managed to get out. The emptiness of the night before crushed me again. She was not with me. Not in any way.

"I'm sorry I don't have more answers for you. We'll have to wait for Meredith to tell us what happened. In her own time."

"In her own time," rang in my head, and for a second, I thought she hadn't lost her memory. How could she forget? Meredith's brain was superior to every other person's I'd ever met. This was part of a game she was playing. Maybe to protect herself. She hadn't really lost her memory. She just wanted everyone to think she did. When I went there, she'd remember me. The same way if I closed my eyes, I knew what her breast felt like beneath my fingertips or what her hair against my face felt like when I whispered, "I love you," in her ear. I remembered every breath, every touch, every moment. She had to, too.

❧

I PULLED IT TOGETHER AND walked the stepping-stones to Jenna's front door. Her oldest son, John, opened it before I even knocked.

"Hi, Chief!"

"Hi there. Is your mom home? Or your dad?"

"Dad's at work, but I'll get Mom." He proceeded to take a half step back from the door and yell, "Mom," at the top of his lungs into the house.

"Stop yelling," a female voice screamed. "For the love of everything holy in this world, please stop yelling."

Jenna came to the door and stood in front of me, shocked. I hadn't been to her house since the day she'd returned from rehab for a leg injury. The time I saw her before that was to charge her with DUI. But I'd known John and Jenna my whole life. It was how this town worked. I'd given her a DUI and then had eaten cake at her homecoming.

24

It really didn't matter what I felt about Jenna, because Meredith loved her. At times, she was the only woman in this town Meredith could stand. I always thought it was because Jenna had alcohol and Meredith had secrets, but after the accident, Jenna sobered up, and Meredith had fallen even more in love with her. Once Meredith had accepted our relationship was possible—that it was real—she loved a lot of things around here.

"Have you heard about Meredith?" I asked.

"No." She hurried to push the screen door out and pulled me inside. "What about her?"

"She fell in her house yesterday. She's in the hospital."

"What the fuck? Why the hell didn't Brad call me?" Jenna was winding up, and her anger showed in her eyes and the tight muscles of her arms.

"I don't know. She's going to be okay, but I wanted to ask you some questions."

"I need to get to the hospital."

"She's sedated right now."

Jenna stared at me, probably wondering why I knew so much. "Questions about what?"

I followed her into the kitchen—the one I'd stood in with Meredith and begged her to reopen her e-mail account so I could talk to her again. The kitchen where I'd told her to just say the word, and I'd be at her side again. The deep burgundy color of the walls covered me with the desperate feeling of being without her.

I won't go through that again.

"How was the Walsh's marriage?" I asked.

Jenna stood perfectly still and watched me. She and Meredith were the kind of friends who'd take a bullet for one another. Women like that didn't discuss each other's marriages with people who knocked on their doors.

I continued, "I'm concerned it wasn't an accident."

That statement broke down her guard. She went from a statue to being lit on fire. "I'll fucking kill him if he hurt her."

"Jenna!" John yelled as he entered the house from the back door. Everyone yelled here.

"Hey, Vince. What's up? Everything okay?" I'd seen the look a thousand times before. My presence, especially in uniform, rarely put people at ease.

"Mer fell yesterday. She's in the hospital," Jenna said and turned back to me.

"Oh, man. Is she going to be all right?" John asked, grabbing a soda from the fridge. He didn't love Meredith the way Jenna and I did. How could he?

Jenna ignored John and crossed her arms. "Brad's a dick, but I don't think he'd ever hurt her."

John walked over, intrigued by the conversation. "Brad would never hurt Meredith." He shrugged the whole idea off. "The only time I've ever seen him pissed at her was when I told him about the Cub Scout campout."

"What about it?" Jenna asked before I had a chance to.

John opened the refrigerator again and stared into it as Jenna and I hung on his every word. "The one Matt got his ass beat at."

"What are you talking about? What Cub Scout campout?" Jenna wasn't used to being in the dark.

John stood up and faced us, leaning on the refrigerator door. "Last spring, Brad was out of town and Meredith brought James to the campout."

"Yeah . . ."

"Right before we put out the fire, Meredith and Matt Thompson were the only people by the bathrooms, and somehow Matt ended up face down on the ground with two black eyes."

"What?" Jenna asked, and I stayed silent, knowing I'd delivered the black eyes when I'd caught Thompson on top of

Meredith. "Why the hell was Brad pissed about that?"

"He was pissed Meredith never said anything about it. And he always thought Thompson was after his wife. Shit like that pisses guys off."

"Meredith doesn't give a fuck about Matt Thompson," Jenna said convincingly to both of us. "The only people she cares about are Liv and James." I could tell there was more. Jenna wasn't telling me everything, but I was afraid I was the rest of it, even if Jenna didn't know it.

"And her husband?" I asked, not really wanting to hear the answer.

"Brad isn't around much. Those kids are her life."

six

Brad Walsh

"I'M GOING TO BE AROUND more," I said to myself as I waited for the kids to close the car doors and follow me into the hospital.

She's awake.

Everything would go back to normal. It would be better than normal. It would be the way it used to be. I'd go tell Dharma we were done, and then I was going to get my house in order, starting with my wife.

When we walked into Meredith's new room, out of the ICU, Liv burst into tears again. Only instead of sadness, they were tears of joy. Meredith faced me and looked exhausted, but then she smiled brightly at the children.

Does she hate me?

She held her arms open, and the kids climbed into bed with her, snuggling in on each side. I started to drag them out, but she said they were perfect just where they were.

"Well, you obviously haven't forgotten these two," the doctor said, smiling at each of the kids.

"How could I?" Meredith pulled them tighter against her sides.

"We're trying to figure out the last thing your mommy remembers. You guys can help," he said and looked my way to draw me into the conversation. The doctor proceeded to ask Meredith the year, which she couldn't answer. The closest she got was that it was post-9/11. She didn't know who the president was, either. I grew more and more anxious with each question she couldn't answer. The doctor didn't appear alarmed. "Do you recall what the weather was like the day you fell? What season it is?"

"I've heard the nurses talking about the heat outside, so I know it's summer." Meredith looked outside to confirm her answer. The sun was shining through the leaves on the tree next to her room.

"How about the winter? When it was cold."

Without moving her head, Meredith's gaze darted around the room, and then she seemed to relax. "The kids got new boots. Liv's are neon pink," she said triumphantly, her thoughts were finally warming up with the exercise. My teeth ground together. I didn't want her to remember everything.

"That wasn't last winter. It was the one before," Liv said, snuggling in closer to her mother.

"We took the kids to Niagara Falls over spring break." She was speaking fast. I could hear the terror in her voice. I lowered my eyes so she couldn't see my satisfaction.

"That was third grade, Mom. I just finished fourth," James corrected her.

"Oh," Meredith said, searching her brilliant mind again for the answers that hid from her.

"We didn't go anywhere this year. Dad was in London."

A sharp pang of guilt shot through my mind and conjured up the image of Dharma kneeling before me in my London hotel suite with my dick in her mouth. I was determined to forget Dharma had happened the same way Meredith had forgotten.

"That's enough for today," Dr. Evans said as he wrote a few notes on Meredith's chart.

"What's happening?" Meredith asked, and everyone looked

at her. She was trapped in darkness, and no one could help pull her out.

"I know it's hard, but give it time. In the vast majority of these cases, a patient's memory will return"

"When can I take her home?" I asked.

"A few days. We're going to run some more tests, and I want her to speak with a therapist." He turned toward Meredith, "See if we can't help speed things up."

Great.

The doctor left me alone with my wife, who was surrounded by our children who showed no sign of letting go of her anytime soon. Over their heads, she mouthed, "I'm scared," to me.

I held her hand in mine and ran my fingers over her wrist. It was bruised with a lump on the center of it. The bruises spread an ugly disgust through my mind and took me back to her body limp on the stairs. The last time she had looked at me, fear filled her eyes. Then her eyes had closed and stayed closed for an entire night, not releasing me from my guilt, not absolving me from my sins.

But Meredith smiled at me now. She was afraid, and I was here to protect her. I was her husband. I raised her wrist to my lips and kissed it.

"Just a bump in the road. We've got this," I said, and it reminded me of the day we'd fought over our wedding. Meredith and I rarely argued. Neither of us found it to be a productive use of time, but she hadn't wanted a big wedding, and I'd insisted on a huge party. I could usually persuade her, but she'd been solid in her determination to just fly away somewhere with me. In the end, I'd won. I always won. After the ceremony, I'd told her it was worth the argument to see her come down the aisle in her gown and rubbed her hand just like this to ease her anger.

"You're going to need help with the children while I'm in here. The babysitter's phone numbers are in my phone."

"Don't worry about a thing. I'm going to take care of

everything, including you and them. I love you, Meredith."

"Mr. Walsh?" a nurse asked as she walked into the room and smiled at James and Liv practically on top of Meredith.

"Yes."

"They need to see you down in billing."

I rubbed my temples and considered the kids. They would drive me insane anywhere near billing.

"You can leave them here. We'll keep an eye on them."

"Thanks."

I took one last look at my children draped over my wife. They loved her more than the air they breathed. Meredith held them tight to her body and stared out the window, and I knew she was searching her mind for the memories that were eluding her. I knew she wouldn't let her brain rest until she remembered.

And all I wanted was for her to forget.

seven

Chief Vincent Pratt

JACK'S GAME WENT INTO EXTRA innings, and I thought I'd lose my mind. I helped Lynn buckle the kids into their seats, and she stopped me at the back of the car.

"What time do you think you'll be home?"

"Not late. I'm going to stop by the hospital to check on Meredith Walsh, and then I'll be back."

"Good. I want to talk to you."

"Okay," I said, and my wife leaned up and kissed me. I watched her climb in the minivan and stepped back as she pulled out of the parking spot. She drove away, and my mind returned to the only thing consuming it all day—Meredith Walsh.

The ride to the hospital felt twelve hours long. Her doctor had called during Jack's game with the update that Meredith didn't recall the accident, and that it appeared she'd lost the entire last year. I'd wanted to drive to the hospital that second and make her remember. I wanted to kiss every inch of her body until she screamed out, "Colonel," and came in my arms. But she wouldn't want that. She'd still insist we be a secret.

I walked into Meredith's room, hoping she was alone, but what I found was her nestled between her two children sleeping on each side of her. They were serene and happy. I knew how they felt. I'd slept one night with her, and it was heaven. One time in an entire year, I'd woken up with her next to me. And these two children were the reason. Meredith refused to upset their peace by leaving their father.

"Hey!" She recognized me. She knew me.

She took my breath away. I couldn't speak. The silence of last night and the stress of today crashed down on me. I wanted to lay my head in her hands and be touched by her, but her children filled the space where I needed to be.

"Hi."

"You're the colonel." Her smile beamed. "I remember you." Her eyes lit, but they weren't with a secret between us. She looked at me the same way she had on the bus ride to Philadelphia. "We were on the field trip together."

"Yes. We were," I said, fighting to keep the lightness in my voice. My memories were intact, and they were pulling me under. "And now we work together."

Her eyes darkened. "Work?"

Hope drained from me. I was lost in the fear in her eyes. Her mind was failing her, and it never had before. "Yes. You work part-time at the police station. You've been there a few weeks now."

"I'm sorry."

"It's okay." I stepped closer to her bed and put my hand on the side, needing to be near her even if I couldn't touch her.

"How could I forget a job?"

"Give it time. It'll all come back."

"Did I interview for it?"

"Yes. With me and the mayor."

She looked out the window and then back at me. "I've never even met the mayor."

I couldn't help myself. I patted her forearm. Grief was moaning in my chest. It was forcing the air from my lungs and

33

pushing me toward her. It dared me to take her. I couldn't stay much longer.

"Do you remember the interview?" She looked down at my hand, but not as if I should remove it, so I didn't.

"Like it was yesterday."

"Why did I say I was interested in the job?"

My God, I just wanted to pick her up and carry her to my car. I wanted her in my hunting cabin, sitting naked on the couch with me the way she had before. I watched my fingers touch her arm. "You said you recently came to realize that a person can change the world in big ways and small ways, and the job was your way for right now."

"Damn, I'm a good interview." She smiled, and the grief in my chest was replaced by Meredith.

"You were the best I've ever had." I choked a little on the last word and steadied myself. My fingers against her arm lightened, and I let a smile spread across my face. I wouldn't let her see the immense truth in my words.

I heard his footsteps in the hall and pulled my hand away at the exact moment Brad Walsh walked into the room. Meredith looked at her arm and up at me. I smiled to put her at ease. I didn't want to frighten her more than she already was, and I didn't want to leave her with her husband.

"I'm going to let you get some rest," I said and then turned to walk out. But I turned back to make sure her husband heard the last part, too. "Everyone can't wait for you to come back to work."

Meredith only smiled, but I could tell she was thinking about the job she couldn't recall. I knew the memory loss was eating away at her. Brad followed me into the hall, and I hoped he followed me all the way outside so I could kick his ass.

"Thanks for coming," he said without an ounce of gratitude in his voice.

How did Meredith stand one day with him?

The more time I spent with him, the less I still wanted him to be alive. "When Meredith's released, I'm taking her away for a few weeks," he said, and I utilized every ounce of training I've ever had not to react.

"Do you really think that's what's best for her?"

"That's none of your business," he said and stared at me, challenging me to refute his statement.

"Where are you going?"

"I'm taking her and the kids to the shore. Give her some time to relax, and give us some time together as a family." He was going to hide her away. He didn't want her to remember, which only made me need to know what happened yesterday in the Walsh house more. What he'd done to her.

"Well, as soon as she gets back, the job will be waiting for her."

"If she still wants it."

I was going to kill him. "Of course," I said and walked away. I had more to do before Brad Walsh died.

❧

I COULD HAVE SLEPT IN my truck when I parked it next to my house. I could have let my head fall back to the seat behind it and gone to sleep, but I didn't. I dwelled on the feeling of Meredith, naked as she straddled me in the small space. She'd fit perfectly between me and the steering wheel. I regretted de-activating the e-mail account, because I needed to hear her. I needed her to know us, and in those e-mails, she did.

I stepped out of the truck and closed the door behind me. My mind raced with an excuse to go see her again tomorrow. I opened the back door, and Lynn was at the kitchen table in her robe, drinking a glass of wine.

She wanted to talk.

"Hi," she said so gently it was as if it came from the wine.

"Hi. Sorry I'm so late."

"You're fine. How's Mrs. Walsh?" Lynn asking about Meredith should have made me sick, but it didn't. Lynn was the kindest person I knew. "She's very lucky." The words left bitterness in my throat. It seemed my luck had run out. "What did you need to talk about?"

Lynn stared down into her wine glass. "I don't think you love me anymore." Her voice was quiet, but her words screamed in my head. They accused me of every sin I'd ever committed, including leaving her alone in this marriage. I'd convinced myself that Lynn was unaware, but now, I realized Meredith and I had never existed outside of our marriages. My love for Meredith was the middle of my world, and that left Lynn some place faraway from there.

I forced myself to face my wife. "I'll always love you. You're the mother of my children."

"That's not what I'm talking about." Lynn ran her fingers around the delicate stem of her glass.

"I know." I was exhausted, and I didn't want to have this conversation, not tonight, anyway. I would have it with her, though. If for no other reason than the fact that she deserved so much more than I had to give her.

"Since Tyler died, you haven't been the same." She took another sip, and I stayed still. "It's been over two years. I've waited for you to come back, but now I think you're not going to." She sighed, and in the dim light of our kitchen, I knew I wasn't coming back.

"I don't know what to say, Lynn."

"Tell me the truth. Is there someone else?" She stared into my eyes, searching for the truth I'd been keeping from her.

"No. Honestly. There's no one else." The absence of any recollection on Meredith's face wounded me again in my memories. "But since Tyler fell over dead on the side of the road, I've felt like both of us deserve more. He was my best friend. He was here, going out for a run, and then, he was gone." Her eyes didn't waver from mine. "If I died tomorrow, would you memorialize me as perfect in your mind, or would you remember all the nights we sat on the couch and watched television without saying a word to each other?" She closed her eyes, and I knew she was going to cry. "There's more out there for both of us."

"Fuck you," she said and stood. She put her wine glass in the sink and walked up to bed.

eight

Brad Walsh

THE DOCTOR THOUGHT MAYBE TWO more days. I scrubbed the blood off the stairs. My arm ached before I got to the second step, and the guilt came back again. I'd searched her closet, her car, every file in her desk, and her checking and credit card statements. It wasn't until I sat in the bank with her empty safe deposit box on the table in front of me that I'd admitted I was crazy. Meredith wasn't the type of woman who'd have an affair. It was beneath her.

This jealousy was because of Dharma, who, no matter how many fucking times I told her not to, continued to text me.

Dumb bitch.

She was going to be gone as soon as I got back to the office. Meredith and I would start fresh. We'd be a team again.

MEREDITH LOOKED WORSE THAN I thought she would when I picked her up from the hospital, and I questioned whether the shore house was a good idea. On our wedding day, her father had told me, "If she's ever in trouble, take her to the water." I'd nodded at his advice but had no clue what the fuck he was talking about. *Should I take her to the shore and baptize her?*

I was just happy to have Meredith. Her mother had said, "You'll never be able to control her. Your only hope is to contain her." I assumed it was more of the rhetoric Meredith hated from her mother. She'd made the woman out to be a dream crusher, the dreaded and droning voice of reality that had sucked the life out of Meredith and her father.

With Liv glued to her side, Meredith moved gingerly from the wheel chair to the Escalade. My wife was pale and unsure of her footing. It was as if losing her memory had disabled her physically. She was still so beautiful, though. On the unmarred side of her head, wisps of hair fell across her face as if she'd been lounging on the beach, letting the wind dry her hair after a swim in the ocean. Her eyes, even exhausted, were still the bright color that changed from blue to green and somewhere in between, depending on what she was wearing and what she was thinking.

She could have died.

I forced the idea from my mind as I helped the kids into the car.

The drive was quiet, and the kids didn't ask any questions. They would have never asked a question again for their mother to be with them, I thought. They were at peace just in her presence.

As soon as I climbed into the car, I took her hand in mine, and as I drove, I sneaked glances at her. We were still on the highway when I saw her eyes drifting shut. She tilted her head toward me, hiding her bruises from the sunlight, and I squeezed her hand to let her know I was there.

When we parked at the house I'd rented for fifteen days, I knew it was the right decision. She needed to be away from our home and away from the memories that threatened to unravel us. I would fill her mind with our children and our marriage as it was meant to be. I would make sure that if—when—the horrible images returned, none of them would matter because

Meredith and I belonged together.

I settled her into a lounge chair on the deck with a perfect view of her beloved Atlantic Ocean. She was nauseated and not interested in dinner, and every move she made, I watched in fear of her memory coming back.

❧

"I FINISHED GETTING THE KIDS set up," I said and walked out onto the deck she was on.

"That's so much work. Did you make all the beds?"

I laughed. "No. I hired people to do all of that and stock the refrigerator."

Meredith smiled at me as if this made much more sense than what she'd originally assumed.

"I invited Jenna and John and the kids down tomorrow."

"Oh . . ." The ocean breeze surrounded us, and she pulled her hoodie up around her neck.

"Don't you want to see her?" I'd secretly love if their friendship ended. Jenna was nothing but trouble.

"I would love to see her. I'm just not sure I'm up to a party." She bit her lip and looked over the railing at the horizon.

"Mer, Jenna doesn't drink anymore."

The terror returned to her eyes. "What?"

"There was an accident. She was driving drunk. She still walks with a slight limp, and she never drinks."

"Oh." The color drained from her face. I'd never seen her so lost. Even after the death of her father, Meredith was never like this. She rested her face in her hands and sobbed. I lifted her legs and rested them on my lap as I sat on the end of her lounge. "How can I not remember that? How can I not know what Santa brought my children for Christmas last year or the song Liv sang in the talent show?"

"You hit your head. Hard."

"Or that! How could I forget that?"

The guilt creeped back up and lodged in the back of my throat. I swallowed it down. "I don't know," I whispered into the wind. I turned back to Meredith and added, "You'll remember everything you need to."

"It's terrifying." Meredith stared out at the ocean. The sun had dipped below the horizon and the only visible part of the water was the breakers crashing on the shore in the darkness.

I needed her to stay with me forever and know how much she loved me. How happy we were the day she'd walked down the aisle. Even if she'd never wanted an aisle in the first place. She had to focus on how we'd laughed during our first dance as husband and wife. I wanted her to have the happy memories, and I wanted her to forget the rest.

"When your father died, I thought it would break you," I said, and she looked back at me with surprise clear on her face as if I'd read her mind, or heard something that was never meant to be said.

"I did, too."

"You amazed me. You were pregnant with James, and you never complained—not once. You never sat down. You never stopped comforting your family and his friends. I kept thinking, 'When I leave this earth, I hope she's still here, because she'll make sure life goes on.'"

"He would never have let me give up."

"And you're not giving up now. We're going to come out of this stronger than we were before." Meredith's eyes lingered on me. The quiet unnerved me. That and what she was thinking in her empty mind. "Just trust me. I'll tell you everything you need to know."

I kissed her and went inside to charge my phone. Meredith sat in silence for the next two hours. I knew without asking that she was trying to force the memories to return, which was exactly why I didn't take her back to our house. The stairs, the foyer, even the swing set might trigger her recollection. I would avoid it as long as I could. I sent an e-mail inviting ten other families for a party at the shore house the next day, and then I ordered food from a local restaurant so she wouldn't worry about cooking. We would make new memories.

MEREDITH WOKE UP WITH A headache, took some pain-killers, and went back to bed for a while. Jenna was the first to arrive. By the time the third family walked through the door, she was shooting daggers at me from her angry eyes.

"Are you a fucking idiot?" Jenna asked, overflowing with disdain. *Are you a drunk?* "She had a hole drilled in her head less than a week ago. She doesn't need—She can't handle a party."

As if she were on my side, Meredith emerged from the bedroom wearing the bikini I'd packed for her and a sheer cover-up. When she saw all the people, she crossed her arms over her chest. *Why cover up?*

Meredith was engulfed by well-wishers, and I realized Jenna was right. It was a lot of people and not everyone was here yet. I didn't care, though. It would also keep Meredith's mind off her mind.

More families showed up, bringing small gifts, get well soon flowers, or kid's beach toys with them. Eventually, when the house got too crowded and too loud, we moved outside. The adults settled in chairs and loungers on the deck, and the kids ran down the small wooden ramp to the beach.

Sarah had Liv take a group picture of all the adults with the ocean behind us. I sat down and pulled Meredith onto my lap. Liv still had the camera, so I asked her to take a picture of us. The new us.

Liv looked at the back of the phone and then at Meredith.

"I love you, Liv," Meredith said, and Liv snapped the picture.

Sarah took her camera back and raved about Liv's photography skills. "I'll text you a copy," she said to Meredith, and

Meredith turned to me.

"Do you know where my phone is?"

"It's in the bedroom, but it needs to be charged."

"You thought of everything."

I kissed her cheek and told her I loved her.

When the party settled down and everyone went home, I took my wife to bed. I watched as she changed out of her bathing suit and brushed her teeth. Even with her hair shaved on one side, she was still the most beautiful woman I'd ever known. I stood behind her at the bathroom sink and pushed her hair to the side. I let my lips fall to her neck, and it reminded me of when we were first married. She stiffened immediately.

"Brad, I'm not—"

"I'll be gentle." I kept my lips moving gently across her skin.

"It's been such a long day. I don't feel well."

"I need you, Meredith. I need *this* tonight." I sounded desperate.

Meredith watched me in the mirror. "Why?" she asked and I lifted my head to face her reflection.

"Why what?"

"Why do you need this tonight?" There was a cold understanding behind her eyes, and I feared she remembered how lovemaking had been for us the past year. How cold and distant we were with each other.

"Because for an entire day, I wasn't sure we'd ever be together again," I said, hoping I sounded sincere.

"Just give me some time."

She walked out of the room.

nine

Chief Vincent Pratt

I SENT HER AN E-MAIL from my work account. What difference did it make at this point? I just wanted her to talk to me. Even if I never touched her again, I needed to know she was okay. The e-mail was returned undeliverable.

I checked Facebook. She was never on there. I searched her name and the recent posts hypnotized me. Sarah Lawson had uploaded several pictures and tagged Meredith in two. She was at the shore. More specifically, she was at a party at the shore. Had he taken her right from the hospital to vacation?

Can the woman rest at all?

The picture ate away at what was left of my sanity. Not the fact that she was down there, but the happiness on her face. She was on Brad's lap with his arms around her, and her smile was filled with love. She was in love with him.

I stared at the picture until it hurt, and then I leaned back in my desk chair and let my focus fall toward the ceiling.

She'll come back.

She would remember being at the Sagemore Resort with me. She'd remember me waiting for her inside her hotel room. How I was the one who opened the door and found her leaning against the wall with her head hanging low as if we were doomed. I'd pulled her inside and trapped her against the wall.

I'd kissed her as if we'd never see each other again. She had to know how much I loved her. She had to know it every day for the rest of our lives.

I'll never be what you want. I shook my head as Meredith's words rang through it. She was wrong. I couldn't want anything but her. I had told her that, and before I'd made love to her, I'd promised, "I'll never ask you for another thing, but just say the word and we'll be together forever." I wouldn't push her for more. I'd forever let her tell me what she needed from us.

I'd wait for her to say the word now. Even if it broke me.

I'D BEEN SLEEPING ON THE couch at my house, and it was killing my back. We'd decided to wait until school started to tell the kids, but it seemed like just the sight of me was killing Lynn. She thought if they had a better routine they wouldn't take our split as hard. I wasn't so sure, but I was in no rush to tell them. Meredith had put the fear of God in me when it came to the damage divorce inflicted on children. I prayed every day this was the one thing she was wrong about.

The house I was standing in needed work in every room. The front porch was literally falling off, but I could fix it. I could fix all of it. I needed a place to stay, and Jackson Serwan would let me stay here rent-free while I worked on it. It was a deal I couldn't pass up.

"So what do you think?" Jackson asked. He was hoping I'd agree.

"It needs a lot of work."

"All work you can do. We can make a fortune off this place."

"We?"

"Well, me. But you'll get to save on rent. You sure you want to do this?" he asked, and it was as close to a real conversation as Jackson and I had ever come close to having.

"I'm sure I need to move out." I looked around at the stained wallpaper. "This place I'm not so sure about."

My phone rang, and as I reached for it, Jackson tossed me the keys and walked out. I guessed that was decided. I answered the call and caught the keys before they hit me in the face.

"Hello," I said, dreading the intrusion on my day off.

"Colonel?"

My heart rose up in my throat. I walked to the window to make sure my reception was good. "Meredith?"

There was a pause, and I thought she'd hung up. I was already turning toward the door. Ready to storm Sarah Lawson's for the address of the shore rental Meredith was trapped at.

"Yes. Sorry. I guess I should call you Chief Pratt."

I exhaled and stood still, trying to slow my heart rate. "Are you all right?" I could hear the need in my voice. I couldn't change it. I couldn't sound normal no matter how hard I tried. And God, I swore, I was trying.

"Yes. Slowly but surely, I'm feeling like my old self. I was actually calling because I'd like to come back to work when the kids start school." I closed my eyes and imagined her for the thousandth time at the receptionist desk at the station. "If it's okay. I'm sure my unexpected absence has been a huge inconvenience."

"No. Not at all. We can't wait for you to return. You can start tomorrow if you'd like."

"Actually, I've been down the shore. It's kind of an imposed vacation for me to rest. I'll be here another whole week."

"Are you feeling better?"

"At first, I felt terrible, but now that everyone has left me here alone, I'm quite bored."

My heart raced in my chest. Meredith and I would have killed for a day alone at the beach before she'd been hurt. "Well, we should probably meet before you come back. I could drive down and bring some lunch if you'd like." Silence.

What am I saying?

"Or not. Whatever's best for you," I added.

"I'd love it. But do you mind if we go out to lunch? I'm starting to get depressed looking at these same four walls."

"That's perfect. Tomorrow okay?"

"Yes. Come whenever. I'll be here." She gave me the address, and I had to hang up. I wanted to hear everything about the last week. I wanted her. But I let her go.

❧

I WAS DRIVING TO THE shore to take Meredith out—in public—for lunch. She may not realize it, but this, a real moment instead of a stolen one, was the one thing that she had longed for more than anything else. I parked in the driveway of the rental at exactly eleven. I knew it was early for lunch, but I couldn't wait. Like, I couldn't wait one more second.

I rang the doorbell and inhaled.

"You're here!" she said as she opened the door. The bruises had faded, her hair was in a ponytail, making it hard to see the damage to her head, and she had a beautiful smile on her lips. She was exquisite. I smiled back without realizing it. She enchanted me. "Come in. You have to see the view." She pulled me through the door, and I followed her up the stairs to the living room of her shore rental.

I looked out the three sets of sliding glass doors facing the ocean. "Wow. That's some view."

"You just missed the dolphins swimming by. I swear they know I'm here," she said and blushed.

"I'm sure they do. They know where all the mermaids are."

Meredith stopped and stared at me. Her eyes searched mine for answers I wasn't going to give unless she demanded them. "How's work?" she asked without looking away from me. She tried to keep me talking. She wanted to hear what I knew. The advantage I had was cruel, but it was the only time I felt I was on equal footing with her.

"Slow, which is good. Where's your family?"

Meredith sighed loudly and then smiled at me again. "My husband was supposed to be here all week, but work called. I think he underestimated what two full weeks with us is like." *Heaven. That's what it's like.* "And my brother took the kids for a few days because he thought I needed time to recover. Which I do." She turned and stared at the water again. "Brad was bored with recuperation, but I'm trying to heal as fast as I can."

"Have any memories returned?"

"A few little things. It's not coming back as the doctor described." I stayed silent, only questioning her with my eyes. "They told me my memory would most likely return in the order of my experiences. That the memory loss would shrink until everything, including the day I got hurt, returned. But so far that's not the case."

I needed her to remember everything from me to what happened that day immediately. "What has come back? Exactly." My breathing was deep. I could see my chest rising, wanting her.

Meredith watched me. I knew she was memorizing every detail of this conversation and of me, hoping to leverage it later against her lost thoughts. "Just a feeling, a song, driving in my car . . . Nothing I can put together to form a coherent memory. It's horrifying. Can you imagine not being able to remember the people you love?"

"No." I didn't know what else to say. I wanted to climb into her head and retrieve her memories for her. I wanted to kiss her and see if it brought her back to me. If I could, I would rip her clothes off and touch her until her memories showed themselves. But for now, I had to be satisfied with standing in her shore house next to her.

ten

Brad Walsh

FINALLY HAVING ESCAPED FROM MY family I drove the highway and considered what the chances were of James having thought "the dumbest thing ever" twice a day? Sometimes three times. "Hey, Dad, I just thought of the dumbest thing ever." James would follow it with some incredibly stupid sequence of events that would never occur in real life but took several sentences to convey. I didn't listen to a single word of it.

I turned up the music in my car and felt the tension disappear. Getting back to work where things were controlled and away from the chaos of my children and injured wife was exactly what I needed.

My cell phone rang, cutting off the music. I answered it and Dharma's voice filled the car.

"Where have you been?"

"I was at the shore for a few days."

"I know, fuck face. I saw it on Facebook. Why the *fuck* haven't you called me?" Her voice rose as she finished the question. Having a cool head was not something Dharma was known for.

"Where did you see it on Facebook?"

"On your wife's page. Why haven't you called?"

Why are you on my wife's page?

"Meredith—"

"Don't say her name to me," she cut me off, and her words tore through my rational plan to end things with her. Dharma was not rational.

I sighed. "My wife fell and was hospitalized. It was a scary few days. When she was released, I took her and my kids to the shore so she could recuperate." I rolled my eyes. I didn't have to answer to Dharma or anyone else about where I'd been. Today was the last day I was going to put up with her shit. "I'm almost to the office. I'll see you there," I said, through with the conversation.

"Yeah, you'll see me, but you won't talk to me."

"Actually, I do need to talk to you."

"Come to my apartment after work." Going to Dharma's apartment was a bad idea. I'd fucked her six ways from Sunday there over the past two years. She was bisexual, an exhibitionist, and she loved toys. Every inch of her place reminded me of sex.

"I was thinking we could go out for a drink. Maybe head to Delaware or somewhere else out of the way." I kept my voice light. I didn't want to piss her off.

"My apartment. Six thirty. Like usual." Dharma wasn't pissed. She was scary.

I parked my car in its assigned spot, took the elevator to the main floor, and then switched elevators to the top. I opened the door to my corner office on the forty-first floor, and it was exactly as I'd left it the week before. The week before I'd suspected my wife of cheating. The week before her head had bounced off our wooden stairs. The week before I'd taken over as the primary caregiver of my children.

"Hey! How's Meredith?" Amit asked and fell into the seat in front of my desk. He was my only peer in the Philadelphia office. Everyone else was beneath me—or under me, as Dharma liked to joke.

"She's much better. Thanks for asking."

"Scary shit, right?"

"She still doesn't remember anything from last year."

"I should come over. She'll remember me." Amit started laughing before he finished. "I'm unforgettable."

"Yeah. In all the wrong ways." I sorted through the pile of papers in the center of my desk.

"I'm glad you're back. This place is boring without you. Not one person acted like a prick the whole time you were gone."

"I'm glad I'm back, too."

Amit took the picture of Liv and James off my desk and examined it as if he'd never seen it before.

"Hey, do your kids ask crazy questions nonstop?" I asked him.

"Like what? They ask a lot of questions."

"Like, *is clear a color* or *why haven't we tried bionics to solve the water shortage problem?*" Amit's eyebrows rose. He shook his head slowly as he thought. "How about, *how fast is a knot; why can't only bad people die a slow, painful death*; or *if a baby gave birth right as it was born, would they be twins?*" Even I had to stop and digest the last one.

Amit's head now shook quickly. "No, man. My kids don't ask any of that."

Figures.

My hopes of the barrage of questions being normal were squashed by the disturbed look on Amit's face. "It sounds like they're wicked smart, though."

"They are." I sighed. "Smart and exhausting."

They have their mother's brain.

eleven

Chief Vincent Pratt

I THOUGHT I COULDN'T LOVE her more, but I did. Without the guilt of an affair and the fear of being caught stifling her, Meredith was playful and funny. She was the Meredith who ate lunch with me naked and snuck pictures of me to hide in her secret file on her phone. She was the woman I was in love with.

"So what have you been up to since the Franklin Institute? Anything with me?" She looked at me with hope as she asked.

I promised I'd never lie to her, but I would. I couldn't share everything we'd done together or what we meant to each other. She'd have to unlock those memories for herself. "We were at the same places a few times."

"Please tell. No matter how boring. It's fascinating to me." She was wearing a long strapless dress. It was white, and her tanned skin made me want to take it off her. She had a lopsided straw hat on that hid the side of her head that was partially shaved. Her eyes were almost as blue as the sky today.

"Let's see. I saw you at the pool once last summer."

Meredith stared past the people at the table next to us and into the street. After a few seconds, she turned back. She was happy again. "Did I ever tell you how I feel about the pool?" It was a test. To see how well I knew her.

"You said you felt trapped there."

She was in shock. Her words came slowly. "I must really trust you. I've never told that to anyone. I think."

"I think so, too." I warmed, and all the secrets between us held me tightly. "And I'm pretty trustworthy."

"Tell me something else. Please!" She was as giddy as a child, and I couldn't deny her a thing.

"You volunteered to chair the Spring Fair Committee for the elementary school."

"I what?"

I laughed at her shock. I'd had the same reaction the night she volunteered. "You did." When the astonishment dissipated from her face, I added, "Your daughter won the costume contest at the Fall Festival last year." Meredith's eyes filled with tears, and I regretted telling her.

"She did? What was she?"

"Umm, an underwater ballerina or something like that."

"That sounds like Liv." The tears fell down her cheeks, and it was almost impossible not to lift her into my lap right there in the restaurant. "What kind of mother can't remember such things?"

"From everything I've seen you're an incredible mother. You'd give up your life for your kids."

"That's all moms." She dismissed me completely.

We finished lunch and stayed at our table until the server's shift changed. Meredith fought me for the bill, and I won. One more benefit of being in public together. She had to let me pay.

I drove her back to her house on the beach and walked her to the door. She stopped halfway up the path. Her back was to me, and when I looked on the ground to see why she'd stopped, she twirled around.

"You were with Richie's dad." I stayed silent, letting her put the pieces together. "At the pool, you were with Richie's dad, sitting at a picnic table." She was elated as the thoughts came back to her, and then she was in my arms. She pulled me to her and repeated near my ear, "You were at the picnic table."

I ached for everything to come back. I laid my hands flat on her back and closed my eyes.

Meredith stepped back awkwardly. She was blushing, and my heart sank back into the darkness. "I'm sorry." She was embarrassed to have touched me. The idea was ridiculous. "If I ask you something, will you promise not to take it the wrong way?"

"Yes."

God, anything.

"Will you stay for dinner?"

"Is there a wrong way to take that?"

She laughed at me. The same small laugh she'd tried to hide when she was falling in love with me, but today, she didn't hide it at all. "I'm not the kind of woman who has an affair." The laughter stopped. It was one of the first things she'd said to me, and I knew it had meant so much to her, but I didn't care. I wanted her more than anything. "But you're the only one who's jogged my memory. Jenna told me stories for hours last week, and it was as if every single one of them was about someone else." She struggled with what she was about to say. "And frankly, my husband wasn't around enough to have a lot of memories to share." She never broke eye contact, but the playfulness drained from her words as if she were ashamed of her last statement.

"I'll stay. If I can ask you something and you promise not to take it the wrong way."

"Anything."

"For now, don't mention this visit to your husband." I still hated the idea of him anywhere near her.

Meredith's eyes fell from mine to my mouth. I knew she was lost in thought, in some internal, moral debate. She finally looked up. "Deal," she said, and I followed her through the house and out to the back deck.

Meredith interrogated me as the sun set over the ocean. I

told her about the Fourth of July Parade and party we were both at, and then I told her about the Lawson's Christmas party. I left out any details of intimacy between us, and nothing seemed to spark a memory. When she became frustrated, we went inside to make dinner.

She opened the refrigerator and leaned over to peer into it. I could see crab cakes, an entire roasted chicken, cut vegetables, and a pizza. The packed shelves were visible even from behind the island in the middle of the room.

"That's a stocked refrigerator."

"My husband is extravagant as a rule." The way she spoke so nonchalantly about him left no doubt she still didn't remember. Our spouses were always off limits, and even though I knew it was unfair, I saw it as an opportunity.

"The two of you seem so different from each other."

"I like to think so."

We both laughed. Complaining about husbands and wives was something we'd never have done before. Meredith would have left me before she'd said a cross word about Brad to me. It would have been one more betrayal, and there were already so many.

"Brad's a good guy. He just has trouble hearing me. He's a bit self-contained."

"Is self-contained like selfish?"

She didn't respond. Instead, she smiled over her shoulder at me as she began to heat oil in the skillet for the crab cakes. "Have I ever met your wife?"

"You have. A few times. You seemed to like her."

She thought about this, too. Even without her facing me, I could tell her beautiful mind was swirling. "Who don't I like?" She turned to me when she asked. She opened a container of ranch dip and a bag of sliced red peppers and placed them on the counter between us. She waited for me to answer, but I wasn't sure what to say. I didn't want to reveal how intimate we were, how much more I knew, and yet, I couldn't disappoint her.

She leaned in until she was very close, and the urge to kiss her was stronger than my resolve to wait for her. Her lips were full and a deep red from the wine she had drunk. If I kissed her, she might remember. If I laid her on top of the island and spread her legs wide, she'd remember.

"I can tell you know a lot about me," she said. "And yet you're holding back." I stayed still as she watched for my re-action. "So, either you hate me and you're being kind." She held me hostage in her stare. "Or something completely differ-ent but equally as startling is going on." Her voice was steady. Meredith was born to uncover the truth, and she didn't let it shake her. Her smile was coercive, and I couldn't look away to save myself.

She was ingenious and observant, and I was trapped, torn between wanting to lay down with her and feeling obligated to blurt out every truth between us. I knew the truth would only unhinge her more. And I loved her.

"I think I should go."

twelve

Brad Walsh

"I SHOULD GO," I SAID to both women staring at me in Dharma's apartment. "I thought we were going to talk." I ignored the other woman and focused only on Dharma. "I need to talk to you."

"I know what you need." Dharma's voice was thick and deep. She was standing in the living room of her apartment wearing only a thong. She'd answered the door like that. I rushed inside, concealing her enormous breasts from anyone in the hallway.

"Dharma," I started, but stopped myself and looked at the girl standing in the bedroom doorway. She wore only a robe and an absent smile on her face.

"She likes to be used," Dharma said. "Don't you, Carrie?"

Carrie untied her robe and rested one hand on the doorway high above her head. The robe fell open, exposing one side of her naked body. I let my eyes linger over her small breasts and the ample black hair between her legs. Dharma was always waxed. She was manufactured in every way. Carrie looked like she'd been dropped here in a taxi from the eighties.

I concentrated again on Dharma. "I should go." I was here to end this, not to add another person to it. My heart raced in my chest as I fought to remember Meredith lying on the lounge chair facing the ocean.

A fresh start.

"You don't have to do a thing, Brad. Just watch."

Instincts shook my head back and forth. I raised my hands up in front of me, but no one was coming near me. Carrie dropped her robe in the doorway and walked over to Dharma. She kneeled at Dharma's feet, and Dharma took off her thong and lifted her leg. She rested her foot on the coffee table next to her. Carrie smiled at me before turning back to Dharma and licking her pussy. I watched, remembering the taste of Dharma on my own lips. It had been there hundreds of times before.

I inhaled deeply as the idea of Carrie's mouth on me forced the air into my lungs. Dharma placed her hand on the back of Carrie's head and I watched. Carrie never paused the assault on Dharma's clit, as if they were the only two people in the room.

My dick was hard. It pressed against my suit pants and throbbed. I shifted, seeking some relief, and Dharma dropped her head back. She moaned and pressed Carrie's face harder into her pussy before raising her head again and staring at me. Her lips parted, and she inhaled deeply, causing her breasts to rise.

"Come here," she said, and my cock pounded. I couldn't breathe. Carrie kept licking, and I craved her lips on my dick. I wanted her to stop the pounding. "Come here, Brad," Dharma beckoned again, and my feet moved toward her without my permission.

Dharma leaned back so she could watch Carrie's mouth on her pussy without her boobs in the way. "She's going to make me come." I nodded and took in another large breath. "She's going to make us come at the same time." Dharma stroked my dick through my pants, and I was lost to her. "That's what we need, Brad. To come at the same time. Now, take off your pants." I watched again as Carrie's tongue flicked against Dharma's clit. I'd never been with two women before. I unzipped my pants and lowered them. Dharma pulled Carrie's head back by her hair, and Carrie licked her lips. I stroked my dick and waited for instructions.

Dharma moved to lay down on her coffee table and shoved Carrie's face against her pussy again. Carrie rose up on knees and sucked some more.

"Get on your knees, Brad. Behind her." I did as I was told. I reached around Carrie's waist, touching her wet pussy with two fingers. This was wrong, and the depravity of it made my dick throb harder. I rubbed my fingers together savoring the feel of Carrie. "Fuck her, Brad. Fuck her until you come." She pressed Carrie's mouth against her. "Fuck her in the ass, because mine is the only pussy you should be fucking." I stopped and watched as Carrie reached behind and placed her finger in her ass. She took it out, never missing a beat on Dharma's clit. "Fuck her, Brad."

I stuffed my dick in Carrie's ass and completely forgot what I needed to talk to Dharma about.

thirteen

Chief Vincent Pratt

I PLUGGED THE TOASTER OVEN in next to the window and frowned. The outlet was so loose the plug practically fell out. The electrical was going to need to be updated along with everything else in the house. I was using the small bedroom at the top of the stairs as my makeshift kitchen. The one downstairs was gutted. I'd dragged a compact refrigerator, a micro-wave, a table with a folding chair, a milk crate, and this toaster oven up here for the time being. It was worse than my dorm room and my first apartment.

Meredith being at the shore was making me insane. I couldn't come up with another excuse to go down there. I couldn't just drive by. The week dragged. I should have con-vinced her to come home when I was there but I hadn't. Almost two full weeks had passed since her injury, but it felt like two years. It was time for her to come home. It was time for her to remember what her home was like.

"Hello," I heard Lynn yelling up the stairs. "Vince, are you up there?"

I left the toaster oven and went into the hallway. Lynn was facing the top of the stairs with horror covering her face. "Come on up," I said, watching as she touched the wallpaper in the foyer and then rubbed her fingers together to clean them.

"So this is where you're living?" she asked when she reached the landing. She walked past me and stuck her head into my kitchen before roaming the hall and peeking into my bedroom. It was the original master with large windows facing the front of the house. The ceiling was falling in the corner, and my twin bed was pushed against the far wall. Watching as she viewed it made it seem much worse than it had an hour ago. "Were things that bad at our house?" She laughed as she said it.

"Of course not." Lynn had loved the old house we'd rented when we were first married, but when it was time to buy, she'd insisted on new. She was tired of all the noises the old house had made. "How are you?"

"I'm not sure. I keep waiting for you to come home from work, but then you don't, and I remember I hate you."

"Lynn—"

"Let me finish." The anger filled her eyes. It sucked the warmth from the room and left us both standing in the cold. "But mostly, I'm confused. Like when I stop hating you for a few minutes, I can't figure out what happened. Why you're doing this." She paused and looked at the floor.

"I'm sorry," was all I could say. I knew it was nowhere near enough. It wasn't too late to fix this, but it was the first time in years it didn't feel broken to me.

"Sorry for what? Because when I try to figure out what happened, the thing I keep coming back to is there must be someone else."

I stayed still. Uncomfortably so. Lynn deserved the truth, but the truth was if Meredith were still a part of my life, I'd still be a part of Lynn's. Meredith would have left me if I left Lynn. The reality was too fucked up to share with her.

"There's no one else." I didn't let the pain that statement caused show on my face. "I promise. I'm here in this glorious mansion alone every night." Lynn's face turned to stone. "What's wrong?"

"If there's no one else, then it's me. You're really just leaving me. I'm the only one to blame." Meredith always said I would be blamed.

"No. It's not your fault. It's all me, Lynn. I wish I could go back in time and—"

"And what?" she screamed. "And not marry me? Not have our children?"

"God no. I wish I could—"

"What?" she snapped, cutting me off. I saw it then. The hate in her eyes was as clear as a winter sky. She hated me. With every cell in her body, my wife hated me.

"I don't know." I wouldn't hurt her anymore. I wouldn't tell her I should never have married her. I wouldn't discount our children in any way. They were my life, now more than ever before.

"Sure you don't." She walked out the bedroom door and ran down the stairs, sending a rush of creaks throughout the house. The sound of the side door slamming caused the walls of the ancient structure to shake. I stood still, looking around the house that should probably have been torn down. Even if I were never with Meredith again, I couldn't be with Lynn. Our separation was right. It just wasn't painless.

I checked my watch. It was nine thirty at night. *What's Brad Walsh doing while his family is away?* I grabbed my keys off the box near my bed and descended the stairs two at a time. I'd just drive by.

MEREDITH'S HOUSE WAS EXACTLY FOUR point eight miles from town in an impressive neighborhood. Meredith didn't like it here. She struggled with being grateful for what she felt others would appreciate, but she'd never wanted.

Each lot was at least an acre and had mature trees surrounding the houses, making it private despite being in a neighborhood. Her house backed up to the woods, which surround the whole development.

I'd trekked through those woods to sneak into her kitchen. I'd wrapped a tarp around myself and rolled over the snow in her back yard so I wouldn't leave footprints. I'd turned off the lights in her house so we couldn't even be seen with a telescope. I'd done everything she'd asked in order to protect her. To protect us.

The neighborhood was a large circle with fifty houses in it. I drove the long way around, and when I approached Meredith's house, Brad was stopped in the opposite direction with his signal on, waiting to turn in his driveway. I blocked it with my truck and lowered my window.

"How's Meredith?" I didn't say hello or ask how he was, because I wanted him to be gone.

"Chief Pratt, you're out late."

"Is she feeling any better? Has she remembered anything?"

Anything besides being with me at the pool. That came back when I saw her at the shore. Did she tell you that?

I hated him.

"It's late. I'm just getting home from work." Brad didn't seem like he was just getting home from work. His hair was a mess, his shirt was buttoned only halfway up, and his eyes were glassy. As much as Meredith wasn't the type to have an affair, Brad absolutely was. And he still hadn't answered my questions.

I ignored his statements. I preferred to ignore him for the rest of my life, but I wasn't going to. He was going to feel my presence every second he was near Meredith. She would never be hurt again. When she remembered . . . when I found out what he'd done to her, he would feel my presence until he begged me for mercy. "Just so we're clear, I'm concerned about Meredith living here."

"What the fuck are you talking about? My wife fell."

I didn't respond. I didn't stop staring at the piece of shit who'd probably never deserved her.

Brad Walsh smiled, and I thought he was drunk. At least slightly. He straightened in his car seat. "If you don't mind, I'd like to enter my property."

I glared at him. When I couldn't stand the sight of him a minute longer, I put my truck in drive and pulled away slowly, watching in the rearview mirror as Brad turned onto his driveway.

fourteen

Brad Walsh

I SLEPT A TOTAL OF twenty minutes last night. Who the fuck did Vincent Pratt think he was? And why was he so concerned with my wife? It didn't make sense. She hadn't worked for him long enough for him to care this much. Were the doctors or the police suspicious of the circumstances surrounding Meredith's injury? Did they have reason to suspect I'd hurt her?

I read the e-mail outlining the travel arrangements for my upcoming trip to London, not digesting the words. I hadn't even been officially questioned. Everyone at the hospital seemed to believe me. It could have happened exactly as I'd said.

They knew nothing.

A knock on my office door was followed by Amit walking in uninvited. "Hey! I know you've been out, and it's total bullshit, but you need to complete the sexual harassment training online. If you don't, New York is never going to stop hounding me." I squeezed my temples, warding off the pain of stupid, online, corporate training videos that were a complete waste of my time. "I know, I know," Amit said. He did know. "But worse than actually completing the training is being the executive sponsor for compliance, so complete it."

"I've got a lot going on. I'm trying to get ready for London in two weeks."

"Look, it's pretty basic. Don't fuck anybody below you. And since you're as high up as they come around here, just don't fuck anyone."

"Right." Images of Dharma's breast blocking air from entering my mouth while she rode me entered my mind.

"Should take about twenty minutes, and then we'll never have to talk about this again."

"Until next year."

"Until next year." Amit nodded and left.

I needed to talk to Dharma. I'd fucked her twice while Meredith was still at the shore. Both times with Carrie, who was still in town. The idea of using another human being wasn't appealing to me, or so I'd thought. The fact that a girl was happiest being used didn't even make much sense, but every time Dharma ordered her to do something to me, my dick got hard. I couldn't explain it. I also couldn't stop doing exactly what Dharma told me to do.

Dharma walked by my office and bounced her eyebrows at me, and I knew I had to get the hell out of there or I'd be at her apartment after work instead of spending the last night at the shore with my wife and children. That was where I wanted to be. It was where I *needed* to be.

I was eating lunch in my office, trying to catch up on the endless list of things I'd missed while I was out with Meredith. Business didn't stop, even if Meredith's memory did. My phone buzzed next to me, and I picked it up, swiping across the screen to read the new text. It was a picture of Dharma's pussy with a dildo hanging out of it. Apparently, Dharma didn't stop either.

She reminded me of myself, unwilling to let anything stand in her way. Except I'd been that way about work, not an executive's dick. I'd seen her in the hall before lunch and had broken the news that I was on my way to the shore right after work.

Within an hour, I'd received the picture. She was wearing the top she had on earlier when I saw her and the picture was clearly taken in the office bathroom, which meant she'd carried a dildo around with her.

That picture was the only excuse I had for not going to the shore right after work.

❧

I LEFT DHARMA'S APARTMENT AND drove to the shore. I was excited to see Meredith, well, more like anxious. The doctor had said her memory could return at any time. I'd pulled him into the hallway and asked if there was a chance it would never return. I was worried, concerned for my wife. The doctor had shown no indication of mistrusting my motives.

I must have read something wrong. Someone suspected something, because the Chief of Police was suddenly all over me, and was asking about the details of Meredith's injury. One of the nurses, the neurologist, maybe even Meredith herself had said something to raise a red flag, and now I needed to lower it.

The kids were at the shore house, too. Meredith's brother had returned them just in time for me to bring them all home. School was starting soon. Dharma would be gone, and Meredith and I were going to start fresh without any distrust or dishonesty. I just had to figure out how to get rid of Dharma.

I parked in the driveway and heard Liv and James playing on the other side of the house. I walked toward the ocean and saw them kicking the soccer ball back and forth on the sand. Meredith was sitting on the deck, watching them.

"Daddy," the kids both yelled and ran over to me. Meredith smiled, appearing genuinely glad I was there. We were a family.

"Hey! How was Uncle Jeff's?" I asked.

They both spoke at the same time. I couldn't understand a word they were saying, and I really didn't care. I just nodded as if they made sense. James finally muzzled Liv with his hand and said, "We're going to the boardwalk tonight."

I turned to Meredith, praying James had it wrong. The boardwalk was a mix of noise, crowds, French fries, and ice cream. *And* it was a dry town, so there was no alcohol. It was hell. "Really?" I asked her.

"Yes. They haven't been all summer, and school starts next week." She looked good. The bruises on her face were healing, and she had her hair styled in a way so I couldn't see the shaved patch. Her skin had bronzed from her weeks in the sun, and her eyes blazed with the colors of the ocean. I walked to the railing and leaned over to her. She kissed me on the lips and leaned back as she exhaled. I let the feel of her lips linger before opening my eyes. With Meredith, I would conquer the world. She was my wife, and she always would be.

"The boardwalk?" I asked, only half joking.

"Yes," she said and then told the kids to go inside and grab their sweatshirts.

I went in and changed my clothes. When I lowered my pants, I saw lipstick on my underwear. At first, I thought it was a red stain, but then the image of Carrie's lips pulling them off my hips while she'd been bound and on her knees in front of me ran through my head like a train before it derailed. I ripped off the underwear and folded them tightly before hiding them in a sheet of paper from my briefcase I crumbled up. I threw the paper in the trash and covered it with the remaining items in the basket. They were strips of toilet paper bundled tightly together. Meredith was on her period. *Great.*

"Daddy, let's go," Liv yelled as I opened the bedroom door, leaving Dharma behind and joining my family.

I drove them to the boardwalk, bought the tickets, and waited while the kids rode the rides. Liv and Meredith went in a boutique and bought Liv new earrings. James and I sat on a bench and watched the people go by. We were exactly how a family should be.

While the four of us ate ice cream, James and Liv chatted about nothing of use. Which super power would you rather have? If you fell out of a plane when it was taking off, would you survive? Would you rather lose a leg or your hearing? Can a bomb blow up a diamond? I let the sight of Meredith drown them out. She had so much patience with them. She wore a new bracelet. A braided white nautical one every store on the boardwalk sold for a dollar.

"Nice bracelet," I said and turned it on her wrist. She held it up so I could see it better.

"We used to call them shark bracelets when I was little. We swore they kept the sharks away."

"It's nice," I said, and then with her wrist still in my hand, I added, "I think you should quit your job." I didn't want her anywhere near the police station or Vincent Pratt. He'd crossed a line at our house the other night.

"What?" Meredith smiled as if the suggestion was almost funny. She scrunched her brow, trying to figure out what I was thinking. She had no idea I was only thinking about how to get her to resign without making anyone suspicious.

"I think you need to rest, and with the kids going back to school, it'll be perfect for you to have some time to yourself."

"I had some time this week, and I was bored. I'm looking forward to going back to work."

I had to stop. I couldn't push. Meredith would know there was a reason. "What makes you think you liked it there?" I asked with an ease to my voice.

"Did I?" She tilted her head, challenging me, but she had no idea of what.

"To be honest, I don't know. You only worked a few hours a week, which is why it shouldn't be a big deal if you stop." She stared at me, deciphering every word I'd just said. "But it's not a big deal if you stay either. I just thought you might enjoy the time off." I kissed her cheek.

"Mom, what's more important? Your brain or your soul?" James asked, and Meredith slowly released me and turned to him.

She looked out to the sea, as if the answer to his question was there. "Maybe your brain." She put her arm around James and pulled him close to her. "But without a soul, there's no need for a brain, because you won't be able to love. And without love, what is there?"

Who cares? screamed in my head. What was with all the questions? I was exhausted from three hours with these two.

"Who would be the next Queen of England if the Queen hadn't had any babies?" Liv asked.

The questions never stopped. They never fucking stopped. They barely stopped for the answers. Half the shit that came out of their mouths, I'd have to search the internet to even answer. I was exhausted. Meredith was beautiful as she explained the English monarchy to our eight-year-old.

fifteen

Chief Vincent Pratt

SCHOOL STARTED. THANK GOD, SCHOOL started. I went to my old house and stood next to Lynn as the kids got on the bus. I took pictures. I waved. I told the kids I loved them. Then, as the bus pulled away, Lynn turned and walked into the house without a word to me.

I should have cared more. I knew a decent man would have been hurt by her silence, but it was Meredith's first day back at the station, and I was consumed with the idea of her sitting outside my office.

Finally.

I started my truck and turned my radio to the classic rock station. It would forever remind me of my pothead girlfriend. Meredith had said classic rock saved her when she was a teenager, during the years following her parents' separation. She used to switch the radio at my cabin to this station whenever she was there, and I let her. I would be happy listening to crickets as entertainment as long as she was next to me.

What music will my kids turn to?

Lynn and I splitting up couldn't be ugly. We had to stick together as their parents, and that meant Lynn was going to have to speak to me again.

When I pulled in the station, I scanned the parking lot for

Meredith's car, but she drove her kids to school much later than the rural bus picked up mine. She'd be at least another half hour. I tried to hide my joy as I said good morning to the other guys.

"Morning, Daniels."

"Morning, Chief. When's Meredith coming in? I can't wait to see the dent in her head."

There were no female officers here. It was just me and seven other men: one close to retirement, two middle-aged, and four young. Meredith was their mother, their daughter, their friend, and their confidant. They adored her almost as much as I did.

"I'm sure she'll be here soon. Keep in mind that it's her first day back."

Daniels's juvenile grin told me he had no intention of going easy on her. "Oh, I know. Been waiting weeks. I guess you have to bash your head in to get an extended leave around here."

The mention of "bashing" drained the smile from my face. I still had no idea what had happened that day in Meredith's house. Or any other day, for that matter. I was the outsider.

"The last time I spoke with her, she still didn't remember anything—including you."

"You guys talking about me?" Meredith asked as she walked through the front foyer and took off her sunglasses. She had on a tight gray skirt, a black silk shirt, and black heels. She'd worn the shoes to the cabin once and had kept them on while I'd made love to her standing up.

I stood up straight and took a deep breath.

"Always talking about you. Welcome back!" Daniels said as he walked over and hugged her. She watched me from his arms. The sadness in her eyes told me everything I needed to know. She didn't know who Daniels was. He took a step back and didn't attempt to hide his examination of her head. Meredith had pulled her hair to the side of her injury and tied it in a loose bun. Pieces were hanging down, making it impossible to notice unless you were looking for it. "How's that hard head of yours?"

"It's getting there. How are you?" Her warmth shone through her eyes and the way she smiled at him. Even if Meredith didn't remember him, she liked him.

"Bored to tears. I'm glad you're back." Daniels picked up his hat and his coffee and headed toward the door. "I'll see you later. I've got to go catch the bad guys."

"Be careful," Meredith said as he nodded and backed out the door.

The woman I was in love with was only five feet in front of me. We were alone. My heart pounded against the wall of my chest, and I was sure she could see it beating. Meredith didn't smile or speak. She peered around each corner of the room and looked at the ceiling, the floor, and at the hallway behind my back.

"Anything familiar?" I asked as she walked past me and into the hallway that led to the interview room. I followed her in there, watching closely as she pulled the handcuffs attached to the table. The ones I'd cuffed her with almost a year ago.

She shook her head.

She was tan from her weeks at the shore, and her hair was streaked with blond highlights. If I didn't know the reason for her unplanned vacation, I'd say she was the picture of health.

"You have to forgive me," she said, and I stayed still leaning against the doorjamb.

"For what?"

"For not knowing a thing about this job. It's going to be like starting over for us."

"I know. I'm fine with that. In fact, I'd like to take you to lunch today for your second first day."

"Oh, lovely. Where should we go?" She was flirting with me, and she could because there was nothing between us.

"How about the golf course here in town?" We'd never been

there together. Actually, aside from our lunch at the shore, we'd never been in public anywhere together. But if there was nothing between us, then there was no reason not to have lunch.

"That sounds perfect."

"This morning, why don't you familiarize yourself with your desk? I left some documents and the schedule for you to review. Maybe something will jog your memory."

"Memory loss is pure torture."

"I can imagine." *It's killing me.* "You'll have to see if you can figure out your password for your e-mail. I don't have that information."

"I'll try a few."

I left her alone after that. I couldn't hang over her. Well, I could, but I didn't want to unnerve her, or worse, make her not like me. Meredith and I had never had a first date. We'd never had a time when we were getting to know each other. We'd been together and trying to figure out how that should work almost the entire time. This was new territory, and I was eager to impress her.

I watched the clock on my computer from eleven fourteen A.M. until eleven forty-five, and I couldn't take it anymore. I'd seen her legs crossed about an hour before and had to talk myself down from going out there and throwing her on top of the desk. At lunch, I was going to talk to her about wearing jeans to work. I wasn't going to survive many more skirts.

"You ready?" I stuck my head out my door.

Meredith was reading the case files that were new since she'd been gone. She held the file up to me. "Did this pharmacy perp work alone?"

"As far as we know. He didn't give anyone up, and he disabled the security cameras as soon as he entered the building." He'd been whacked out on drugs for most of the interview. We were waiting for him to detox before we took another run at him. "Why?"

"I was just looking at the list of stolen items." She turned the pages in the file, finding the one she was referencing. "Oxycodone, hydrocodone, and methadone." She turned to the next page. "Syringes, eye drops, gauze."

"And?"

"And nail polish." I watched as her mind sifted through the details.

I took the file from her hand and read the list myself. "Interesting."

"Very, very interesting. I already love this job." She was beaming with pleasure. Meredith had found a place to use her mind. The one she'd left with the Department of Justice when she'd quit to raise her children.

"Let's go to lunch."

We walked out, leaving Officer Schlichter there until Daniels returned. Between the two officers, there shouldn't be anything to worry about at the station, and Meredith and I could take a long lunch. It was something we'd never have done before her accident.

"Want me to drive, or are you going to take me in the police cruiser?" Sex dripped from her lips. She was tormenting me. I stopped moving. My heart raced in my chest. Hope burst in my mind. She remembered. I swore she did, but she was as innocent as she'd been when she walked in that morning.

"You can drive," I said. I wasn't sure if I could control myself with her near the hood of my car. I climbed in the Escalade she hated and buckled my seatbelt. Meredith did the same, but before she started the car, she turned to me.

"Did I like working for you?" She was smiling, playing with me the way she always did with Daniels.

"You did," I said and smiled back at her. She was impossible not to be happy around.

"Don't lie. Because I'll ask the others, and they'll tell me."

"I would never lie. You told me you loved me." I turned

away and stared out the window. I knew she was smiling, half-laughing at my words, but I couldn't see her. Or I couldn't let her see how much her words had meant to me.

sixteen

Brad Walsh

"I LOVE YOU," DHARMA SAID. She looked like she may cry, which was impossible because Dharma only had one emotion—need. The declaration, words of adoration spoken by people all over the world, sent terror to my bones.

"What do you mean?" I asked, knowing I should respond but completely void of the words she hoped to hear.

She unbuttoned my shirt and slid it off my shoulders. With the hem of my undershirt in her hands, she said, "I love you. You can't be surprised. We've been together almost two years." She lifted my shirt up and over my head. Her fingertips trailed down my stomach to the top of my pants.

I didn't need this right now. Meredith was just coming around. We were talking again and spending more time together. She still hadn't remembered anything significant, and I'd lulled myself into the safe idea that she never would. The more time I spent with my wife, the less time I had to spend with Dharma. And that was taking a toll. Dharma was used to getting whatever she demanded.

"I don't want to hurt you, Dharma." I kept my hands by my sides.

She slipped two fingers into the waistband of my pants and moved them back and forth, playing with the hair above my dick. "You couldn't hurt me, Brad," she said, and a twisted unease invaded me. I was supposed to be at a work happy hour. I was supposed to be ending things with Dharma. I was *supposed* to be starting a new life with my wife. "Unless I asked you to."

Dharma stroked my dick through the fabric of my pants, and it hardened. She could look at it and make it hard. I'd stuck it in every hole on her body. She begged, she teased, she'd bitten me once. She was like a dirty movie that played for me whenever I turned her on, and Dharma was always on. She reached lower and cupped my balls, and I opened my mouth for more air. I was here to end this.

"Wait here." She took her hand away, and thoughts of my family registered in my mind. "I bought us something." Those thoughts were replaced by butt plugs, ball gags, anal beads, and nipple clamps. *Fucking Dharma.* She emerged from her bedroom carrying a tripod with a small camcorder hooked on top of it. "I want us to make a movie."

My head shook before I could form words. It was unquestionably a bad idea. No pictures. No movies. I wasn't a fucking idiot. I was older and wiser than her. By about fifteen years.

"No?" She wasn't hurt. She wasn't listening. "How about this?" She pointed the camera down toward the couch and pulled me over near it, but out of the line of the lens. "How about . . ." She kissed my neck and unbuttoned my pants. I held on to the tension. No video. No pictures. "I make a video of me, and you just watch?"

Dharma took my nipple between her teeth and bit it as I watched. I winced, and she released it, soothing it with her soft tongue as she caressed the top of my dick.

Just watching can't hurt.

She pushed my pants down and then backed me up until the back of my legs hit the couch. She forced me down and away from the camera angle before taking off the suit she'd worn to the office. She left on her garter belt and hosiery. She wasn't wearing panties.

"No underwear today," she said to me and the camera. "It was a problem. I was wet every time you walked by." I stayed quiet, but my hand reached for my dick and I stroked it. I lifted it up, freeing my balls, and rubbed them too. Dharma watched. She moaned and inhaled deeply at the sight of me jerking myself off, so I slowed down. She wasn't the only one who could tease. Her eyes darted to mine. I would pay for that.

She moved slowly. She was a bitch. She played with her clit and stuck her fingers in herself and then pulled them out and put them in her mouth. She sucked them and watched me before turning toward the camera. My dick throbbed in my hand. Dharma grabbed her breasts. She pinched her nipples and then dropped one hand back to her pussy. She moaned with her lips shut, the way she always did before she came.

Fuck it.

I climbed between her legs and fucked her until I came so hard I thought it would come out her mouth.

I dropped my head to her chest, keeping it shielded from the camera.

Dharma ran her hands through my hair and said, "I love you," and a chill ran down my back.

৹৶

THINGS HADN'T GONE AS I'D planned with Dharma. They hadn't gone as planned with Meredith either. We'd been home from the shore four days, and every minute I was with her in our house, I watched her. I needed to know if she remembered before she did. I filled the quiet with the memories I wished she'd recall. I used the time after the kids went to bed to talk. To remind her of how much we meant to each other.

"Isn't this nice?" I asked Meredith and poured her a glass of wine.

"It's nice . . ." I felt this same hesitation from her a hundred times before. Things weren't as perfect for Meredith as they were in my mind.

"What?"

"It's just you don't always seem like you hear me," she said taking the glass of wine I held out for her.

"Of course I hear you. I hear every word you say."

"Sometimes you go on the defensive rather than really listening to what I'm saying."

"Like when?"

"Like right now." She kissed me lightly on the lips to soften the blow.

I pulled her close to me. "Okay, Meredith. You have my full attention."

Meredith studied me. She was considering her next statement too much. "We should sell the house," she said, and the surprise I knew was on my face was no act. It came out of nowhere.

"What house?"

"This house."

"You love this house," I said. How could anyone not? It was beautiful.

"No. *You* love this house. I don't like it at all. It's too big. Too sterile. I want something . . . warm."

I took a deep breath. I wanted her. I wouldn't lose her, and getting her out of the house might help stifle her memory. But what the fuck? I loved this house.

"Okay. Start looking for a new house."

Meredith hugged me, and I pulled her close. I rested my chin on her head and wished we could stay in this one moment forever. Without the rest of the world fucking things up. "Thank you. You have no idea how much this means to me," she said.

I kissed her. She had no idea how much she meant to me.

seventeen

Chief Vincent Pratt

THE SUIT HANGING ON THE coat rack in my office was a dark cloud over my day. I'd wear it to the school board meeting tonight to watch Vincent Jr. get his student of the month award, and then I'd have dinner with his mother and my parents. They'd all wonder what was wrong with me, and question why I couldn't be the same man I was two years ago. My father was going to pull me aside and ask if I wanted to talk about it. He'd tell me how much they loved Lynn and how worried they were.

I listened as Meredith packed up her things. Even if she never spent another day with me, I couldn't stay with Lynn. It wasn't fair. Lynn deserved someone who couldn't be away from her the way being away from Meredith was breaking me. She deserved more than I'd ever given her.

"See you tomorrow, Chief," Meredith said as she stuck her head in my office. I could only see half her body. One slender leg atop a gray high heel was enough for me to want to attack her. She wore a wrap dress that was perfectly professional, but her body made every piece of clothing seductive. She could be wearing jeans and an oversized sweater, and if she walked by me, I'd become aroused.

"I'm right behind you. See you tomorrow."

When she turned and walked out, I exhaled a huge sigh.

When is this going to end?

What if it never ends?

I pulled up Google, and for the hundredth time searched amnesia. I had read so much about it I could diagnose and treat it myself. I wanted to climb inside her brain and know what she was thinking. She was always jovial, kind, and professional in the office. She treated me the same way she treated the other officers, and it was agony.

After a half hour of reading the same unhelpful articles, I stood and closed my office door. I changed my pants, but looked at the rest of the suit, which annoyed me for some reason it wasn't a part of. I pulled the plastic up and over the shoulders of my shirt and jacket. The dress shirt was starched crisp and the dry cleaner had ironed the cuffs to perfection. It was rough against my shoulders. As I struggled with the button on the cuff, my office door opened and Meredith rushed in.

"Sorry, I took these by mistake somehow—" She stood, just inside my office, with my car keys in her hand. Her eyes fell on my bare chest and she began to sway. She raised her hands to her forehead as if she were in pain.

I rushed over to her. "Are you okay?" I wrapped my arms around her waist to support her and shoved the door closed. "Mar, what is it?"

"Shhh," she said and closed her eyes. She let her hands fall to my chest, where her fingertips stretched across my skin. She stopped breathing, and every cell in my body stood at attention for her. Weeks of not touching her all seemed worth it as she stood in my arms. Her hands on me pulling me to the needs I'd silenced, making it impossible to stay away from her.

I waited. Waited for her to breathe again. Frustration covered her face as a tear fell from her still-closed eyes and she lowered her forehead to my chest. I held her close, never wanting to let her go.

I inhaled her and closed my own eyes. She had to come back to me.

"It's like a blanket wraps around me, holds me tight with intense memories, and then is ripped away, leaving me grasping at frayed threads to keep it." She raised her head, and against my instincts, I loosened my arms around her. She wiped the tears from her face. "I'm sorry." She shook her head as if she was absurd, but she was mine. When she lowered her head once more, clearly angry with herself for not remembering, I pulled her close to my chest again.

"You're going to remember," I said, as much to myself as to her. She had to. I was tired of living without her.

Meredith Walsh

eighteen

IT WAS TERRIFYING. NO MATTER what I did, I couldn't force my mind to comply with my demands. The memories didn't come back the way the doctor said they would. It wasn't a slow shrinking of the missing time. The first thing I remembered was only a feeling.

I was at the shore house Brad had rented to help me recuperate and relax. I wasn't sure where he'd gotten the idea that recuperation should take place during a party, but that was what he did. He took me away from my home and threw a party. I told myself he didn't know what to do and that he was trying, but when Jenna looked at me and rolled her eyes while Brad laughed loudly off to the side, I knew it wasn't all in my head. That brought me back to what wasn't in my head.

As soon as I got Jenna alone, I began the interrogation. If anyone knew what was going on in my life, she did.

"What was last year like?"

"I don't know," Jenna said and took a sip of her water. It was strange to see her without a drink in her hand.

"What do you mean you don't know?" She was my only hope.

"I mean, I don't know. Something was going on with you, but you never told me what. You went through weeks where you were miserable, then happy, and then distant. You were all over the place."

"Was I depressed?" I watched Liv and James running in the sand with a kite. Had I not loved being with them?

"I think so. For some of the time." My gaze circled the room as I searched my mind for memories of sadness. "You asked some strange questions."

"Like what?"

"Like if I ever had an affair." Jenna watched my reaction. She waited, but there was none. "And if John is the only guy I'd ever had sex with."

My head snapped up in surprise. "That is an odd question."

"I know. Any of this coming back?"

"No," I answered honestly. None of it sounded familiar or like the version of myself I knew. It didn't make sense.

When Jenna and the rest of the town finally left, Brad came into the bathroom as I brushed my teeth. He kissed the back of my neck, and it brought back a memory of sorts. It was more of a feeling than a memory.

The feeling of wanting to disappear.

It was a dull ache that swarmed my body, forcing me down and making me crave an escape. The sensation was so strong, I almost told Brad about it, but when I walked out of the room, it lessened. It must have been a mistake. My memories were confused. Why would I want to disappear from Brad? If anything, I should have been clinging to him. He was the only person alive who knew more about me than I did. Yet, he didn't know I wanted to disappear, and I didn't tell him.

A few days later, my brother took the children to his house and Brad returned to work, leaving me alone to battle with my mind. Not having my memory was unacceptable. I searched every megabyte of my phone. I might have lost my memory, but my phone hadn't. I looked through the photo album, the texts, the web history, and all my e-mails. Nothing told a story of anything other than a mother scheduling her children's lives.

I searched through my Facebook page and the page of every

person I knew. I viewed their photos, their posts, their vacations. I'd been to a pony party, the pool, the Fall Festival, and apparently Lacey's mom's shore house and her Christmas party. I was tagged on dozens of pictures of my children. My page had fewer than ten photos of me, and a hundred of Liv and James. Even my profile picture was of the two of them. Brad was nowhere to be found.

I went through every contact on my phone, one by one. Every single one of them was silent regarding the last year of my life, until I found the two entries for Jenna: one with her first and last name and her phone number, and a second entry with her full name, including her middle initial. That phone number was different from the one I recognized, so I called it, and the colonel answered.

I recognized his voice. I knew it was him, but I only remembered seeing him twice in my life. Once on a school bus to Philadelphia and then in my hospital room, but he was on the other end of the phone in my hand. Even across the miles between my hometown and me, his voice warmed me immediately. Instead of hanging up, I made up an excuse for the pause and the phone call. I wanted to return to work. Yes. It was a good one. The colonel was more than willing to come discuss the job and rescue me from my boredom at the shore. He was kind, and I was confused. I didn't know how he fit into the last year of my life or why I'd hidden his number in my phone.

I OPENED THE DOOR TO the shore house, and the colonel was standing on the other side. Every emotion and dirty thought from Liv's field trip to Philadelphia came back. In the hospital, I'd remembered who he was and where I'd met him. But there, standing in the family room of the shore house Brad had rented, as I watched the colonel looking at the view, I knew how sitting next to him on the school bus had made me *feel*.

How my heart had raced as our legs touched. How I'd inhaled the hint of mahogany that followed him and made me want him to steal me away. He was strong and he was kind. It was a compelling combination.

"Wow. That's some view," the coronel said and looked out the three sets of sliding glass doors. The mahogany drowned out the salt air trapped in the house. I inhaled, deeply and silently. I was warm.

"You just missed the dolphins swimming by. I swear they know I'm here," I said and realized what a fool I must have sounded like, talking about the dolphins as if they were my friends.

"I'm sure they do. They know where all the mermaids are," he said, and I stopped breathing. He'd called me a mermaid, but I'd never told anyone about believing I was one. No one except my father. I stared deep into the colonel's light green eyes, waiting for them to reveal what else he knew, but he stayed still, keeping the rest from me. Suddenly, nothing seemed as perfect and simple as Brad had made it out to be.

The colonel visiting me was confusing. He had asked me not to tell my husband about it. I did as he asked and didn't mention the visit to Brad, but that night, I dreamed of the colonel. In the dream, we were having sex, and when I woke up, I thought it was a memory, but that was crazy.

nineteen

BRAD DROVE THE KIDS AND I home, and our marriage was completely different than I remembered it. He was still selfish. That would never change. But he was needy. No, he was desperate and careful, neither of which I'd ever seen in him before. He never spoke of the accident. In fact, he never talked about anything except how perfect we were together. He was attentive and engaged. He asked me questions and appeared to listen to the answers.

I wasn't clear on the last twelve months, but I was certain something had happened to make Brad appreciate me more. Buoyed by this security, I asked him to sell the house, and as soon as the words left my mouth, I felt a relief. It was a burden I'd carried with me that I didn't realize was so heavy. Like a dog lying on a nail, I wasn't aware of the pain until I'd finally stood up.

HOUSE HUNTING WASN'T AS PLEASANT. One might have thought I was taking Brad to donate a kidney. He even asked me to drive. He was acting as if he was so sickened by the idea of moving that he couldn't trust himself behind the wheel. I rolled my eyes as he climbed into the Escalade and rested his head on the window.

"You did agree to this," I said, reminding him I wasn't

making him do anything.

"I regret it." I stopped the car halfway out of the garage and stared at him until he turned to me. "What? I do. Our house is perfect."

"You're never at our house. I'm here all the time." Brad took my hand in his. He'd held my hand through so much in this life. We'd get through this. "Try to keep an open mind."

He raised my hand to his lips and kissed it. "Okay, but only because I want you to be happy."

How could we be so far apart on this? On everything?

We drove the five miles to the brick home set back off the road and parked next to our realtor.

Brad surveyed the green acres of hills surrounding us. Not a person in sight. "Please say we're just meeting him here. That this isn't the house."

"Open. Mind." I raised my eyebrows at him.

I wanted to buy the house just from the outside. It was brick on all four sides with a matching detached garage. Brad looked like he'd eaten bad shellfish for breakfast.

"It was built in seventeen fifty two as a tavern," the real estate agent explained as we strolled up the front walk. I was hanging on every word, and Brad was lagging behind as if he were a dog I was dragging to the vet. We stopped to wait for him at the enormous wooden front door.

"It's impressive," I said, more to Brad than the realtor.

The front door opened into a large room that had an arched opening into the kitchen behind it. My adoration wandered over the floorboards, the stained glass accent panels in the windows, the hearth . . . I was in love.

"This was the original tavern. The fireplace is wood burning and the floors are plank pine and thought to be original."

I touched the windowsill and felt like I'd stepped back in time.

Brad followed our realtor into the kitchen. I heard him say,

"The kitchen was renovated in the nineties. You may want to put your own stamp on it."

I could barely drag myself from the tavern, and it didn't matter what the rest of the house looked like—I loved its story.

The original banister led to three sufficient bedrooms and two baths on the second floor.

"Two?" Brad said to me.

"There are only four of us, and there's a half bath on the first floor."

We followed our realtor to the basement, which consisted of cracked walls and a dirt floor on the southern half.

"You've got to be joking," Brad muttered under his breath.

In the alcove under the stairs stood an artificial Christmas tree, completely decorated and ready to be plugged in. Shiny red balls hung from almost every branch on the tree. It reminded me of a blood splatter. My thoughts lingered on the crime scene Christmas tree.

"What did I give you for Christmas last year?" I asked, not caring if it sounded crazy.

"You got me a new suitcase and put pictures of the kids on the inside so when I'm away, they're still with me."

That's nice.

I was satisfied with the gift. Brad kissed my cheek and followed the realtor up the steps.

"What did you get me?"

He stopped halfway up and came back down to me. Without hesitation he answered, "You asked for an expensive purse, so I gave you five hundred dollars to get it."

"Wow. That's some purse."

"Yes. And it doesn't want to be closeted here."

"I'm sure it'll be fine." I followed Brad upstairs and took one last look at the fireplace in the great room. An ornately carved, wood frame hung on the wall with a certificate of marriage in it. Elizabeth England married Horace Kragler on the eighteenth of June eighteen forty-two, and the address was where we stood. "Is this?" I turned to the realtor, not sure if I was reading the document correctly.

"Yes. At some point, Quakers bought the tavern and used it as a meetinghouse. That's a marriage license from a ceremony that took place here."

This house was the most wonderful residence in New Jersey. I turned around again, trying to memorize every extraordinary corner. Brad was engrossed in his phone. He finally realized he wasn't alone and came to look at the marriage certificate.

"You said you wanted to go to church," I said.

Brad stopped a few inches from me and stared, holding his breath.

Church, Cub Scouts, the book club, a donut, the colonel and his wife. It all came back to me, and then it was gone. Not forgotten, just left alone.

"We went to church for Scout Sunday," I said aloud, and Brad stood completely still. "Didn't we?"

"Yes." I couldn't read an emotion from him. No relief or excitement. He was solid and closed off.

Brad was quiet the whole way home. I cursed my mind for not giving me more. It was almost a snapshot. I couldn't remember the sermon or the presentation of the scouts. It was as if we'd been there, but I hadn't listened to a word that was said.

I went upstairs to change my clothes. I stood in my cavernous closet, hunting for jeans and a shirt to put on. The purses hanging on the wall caught my eye, and I touched each one as I searched for the luxury item from last Christmas.

None of the bags was worth anywhere near five hundred dollars. I must have stored it some place special. Maybe it was in a dust bag on a shelf? I looked from the floor to the ceiling and all around me. I was still searching when Brad walked into our bedroom. He was quiet and looked . . . smaller than normal, almost defeated. The guilt crept up on me in my closet. I felt hollow for loving the house that he hated.

"Hey, Brad, which purse did I get for Christmas last year?"

He leaned into my closet without changing his dismal expression. He pointed to the top purse. It was gray pleather with red piping around the outside and a cheap red zipper. "This one."

"Oh. Of course." Brad left me alone in my closet, trying to figure out the lies I couldn't reconcile.

twenty

I LOVED MY JOB. LIKE, every single day I loved it. I loved packing my lunch. I loved getting dressed and putting on make-up. I loved talking to the officers about their cases. I loved every time they brought an interview into the station.

Today, I loved the deep periwinkle dress I'd bought for work. I couldn't remember the last time I purchased "work clothes," but then again, I couldn't remember a lot of things. I'd worn a black wrap dress last week that was hanging in my closet, and I didn't recognize it so it must have been new for the job, too. The colonel seemed uncomfortable with it. I wasn't sure if it was too casual. It was hard to judge the dress code, since I was the only woman and the only person not in uniform. This dress was beautifully tailored with a V-neck, cap sleeves, and a hem-line to my knee. I would have worn it to court, so it should have sufficed at work.

I walked through the station door to silence. This was typi-cal. Most days it was only the colonel and maybe one other of-ficer there. I dropped my bag on my chair and carried my lunch to the refrigerator in the break room. The colonel was pouring himself a cup of coffee, and he almost spilled it at the sight of me.

"Sorry. I didn't mean to startle you."

He stared at me. His eyes darted to the hem of my dress and back up again so fast I thought I'd imagined it. "No." He shook his head, clearly ridding himself of the images, and I questioned what could be wrong with my dress. "You didn't." He smiled and put me at ease.

"The nights are getting cooler. I slept with all the windows open last night. Best night's sleep in months." The dream of his naked chest hovering above me as he thrust into me replayed in my mind. I lifted my hands to my face to cover the blush that I was sure covered my cheeks.

The colonel was still hesitant. Our usual banter was gone, and I missed it. "I think," I said and waited for him to laugh. When he did, I felt at ease again. I didn't recall my boss at the Department of Justice having this much influence on my emotions.

"I was out in your development yesterday," he said and took a sip of his coffee.

"You were? You should have stopped by."

This he found funny, too, but he didn't explain. "I saw the For Sale sign at your house. Are you going somewhere?"

"Oh, I hope so."

The colonel lowered his eyes, hiding his thoughts from me. "Where?" he asked and cleared his throat.

"Nowhere really. Just a new house. We're looking around here for something less."

"Less what?"

"Less everything," I said, and the colonel nodded as if he completely understood. "You and Lynn should come check out our house. You might like it." I lost him again. His face turned to stone. "It has this crazy irrigation system that measures the rainfall and turns the sprinklers on automatically." I said it jokingly, but he didn't smile. "The grass really is greener at my house."

After the silent equivalent of three hours, he said, "Lynn and I have separated," and I felt the floor dropped beneath us.

It took several seconds of me watching him, and him

waiting for my reaction, for me to process the statement.

"I'm so sorry," I said and shook my head. "How are you?"

"It's been a few weeks. I'm getting used to it."

"How's Lynn? And the kids? You can tell me to shut up and mind my own business at any time." I moved closer to him, fighting a crazy urge to hug him even though he was my boss and the chief of police.

"You're fine. And I think Lynn and the kids are fine, too."

"Can I take you to lunch?" I asked and immediately regretted it.

What do you get for cancer, Meredith? Dinner and a movie.

The man didn't want to go to lunch. "Or not. I can turn around and leave the same way I came in." I nodded toward the door. "No offense will be taken." My discomfort with the subject of divorce surprised even me.

The colonel smiled and half laughed at me. "You can take me to lunch."

⌒⌒

I TRIED NOT TO TALK to him the rest of the morning. I was terrified I might possibly find a topic more intrusive and hurtful than I'd already stumbled upon. When Daniels walked in, the colonel held the door for me, and we walked out into the October sunshine.

"Where would you like to go?" I asked, pulling my keys out of my bag.

"I'll drive. I want to show you something."

"Ooh, sounds intriguing."

The colonel opened my door for me, and I watched every move his arms made. My body warmed from his closeness, and I purposely avoided making eye contact with him. I climbed into his truck with a hand from him. Without the ridiculous running boards on the Escalade, the sheath was a challenge.

"Thanks. This dress."

98

He got in the driver's side and paused as I buckled my seat-belt. "You know, you don't have to dress so nice to work."

I turned to him without saying a word.

Why? Is it inappropriate? Do I not look professional?

I peered at the hem of my dress. It was fine. I let the silence in the truck fill me. I needed it to replace the empty hole his criticism had left.

"Do me a favor?" he asked, and I nodded, looking back up at him. "Forget I said that. Without any explanation, just forget you ever heard the words come from my mouth." His mouth mesmerized me, and I stopped breathing for a moment as I imagined him kissing me the way he had in my dreams.

"Okay," I said. My voice was low due to the lack of air in my lungs. "Forgetting is my specialty."

The colonel drove us three blocks and made a right onto a quaint street near the center of town. He pulled into the drive-way of a dilapidated two-story Victorian. When he took the key from the ignition and stepped out of the truck, I opened my door. He was there with a hand to help me out before I'd turned to the side.

"Thanks." My sight ran over the wooden planks resting on a slant, presumably holding the front porch up. The paint was chipped, the gutters were hanging off, and the window by the driveway was cracked. "Are they serving lunch here?"

"No. Watch your step." The colonel led the way up the side stairs and opened the door with a key. He let the door swing inward and waved his hand for me to go first. Always the gentleman.

I walked into a room, maybe? It was covered in dust, the wallpaper hung off two walls, and the ceiling was caved in at one corner. The past was everywhere.

"When I'm done, this and the room behind it will be the kitchen." He pointed to the back of the house.

"You're renovating this?" I stepped into the front room with the window seat below the bay window. The doorway was double wide, and when I looked at the molding, I realized there were pocket doors that met in the middle. I lifted the door pull and slid the door out. It came *all* the way out and landed on the floor. The colonel and I rushed to grab it before it fell flat. I closed my eyes. "I am so sorry."

"You realize I'm trying to improve this house, not tear it apart."

"Yes." I nodded my head.

He leaned the door against the wall with a kindhearted smile and motioned toward the hallway. "I'm going to open this all up."

I stopped listening when I got to the staircase. "Wow."

The colonel looked up at it, too. "I know. It pretty much sold me on the project." The stairs were wider at the bottom, fanning out and then following the ornate banister up to the second floor.

"Can I go up there?" I almost expected to fall right through to the basement by the fourth step.

"I do it every day."

I let the reality of his words sink in. "You're living here, too?"

"Some version of that. You'll see." It was the saddest thing I'd ever heard from him, but the colonel seemed almost excited about the news. I walked up the stairs and waited for him to lead me into the second floor rooms. There was one obviously set up as a kitchen, although it barely had more than the break room at the station, a bathroom with a sink so small only his tooth brush fit on the side, and a giant bedroom with a small bed pushed up against the wall. The house was a lot to take in, and I suddenly felt dizzy. I didn't know what to say.

"You don't seem impressed," he said. He was standing right next to me. I could feel the heat from his skin and his silent strength that always soothed me when he was in the station. I had to force my eyes to remain open and not let my mind get lost in him.

"Are you happy?"

He stepped farther into the room. "I would be lying if I claimed this hasn't been hard. Everyone around me is trying to figure out who I am and what happened to the Vince they knew. But for the first time in my life, I have such clarity."

"You're the exact opposite of me." Everyone around me knew exactly who I was, and I had no idea.

"From what I know of you, Mar—Meredith, you've always known exactly who you are." The statement made him sad, and it made me want to ask him what else he knew about me. "Just follow your heart. It'll lead you home."

"What if my heart lost its memory, too?"

twenty-one

"MOMMY, HOW FAR AWAY IS Hawaii?" Liv asked.

"Um, probably about five thousand miles. It takes over eleven hours to fly there."

"How far away is Alaska?" she then asked.

"How far away is the sun?" James chimed in, and before I had a chance to answer, he asked, "How far away is infinity?"

I inhaled deeply as I continued to drive the country road to our home.

"Mom?" James yelled from the third row of the Escalade, not letting me off the hook.

"Infinity isn't a place," I started and turned down the radio. "It's an . . . idea. A concept."

"Like love?" James was hanging on my every word, ramping up the pressure of my answer.

"No. Different than love. Infinity is simple. It just goes on forever."

"Like love," Liv chimed in.

"Think of it this way. An infinite love is one that goes on forever. It never stops." I watched as both kids digested my explanation, already dreading any follow-up questions.

"So what's infinity plus one?" James asked, and I considered just pulling over and running from the car.

"You tell me. What's infinity plus one?"

"Infinity," Liv and James both said at the same time.

"What's a googol?" James asked before I had time to recover.

"Hey, I'm going to play some music. I want you to search on Google for what a googol is when we get home." I turned up the music, and Liv sang the wrong words the rest of the way home.

Brad's car in the garage bay next to mine surprised me. It was seven thirty at night and kind of early for him to be home on a Friday. The kids ran inside, calling his name and searching for him. Brad being home before us on any night was a foreign concept to our children, too.

I was the one who finally found him. He was sitting on the back deck, drinking a beer and smoking a cigar. I saw him there but didn't go outside. I watched him from the back door, scouring my mind for the sensation of loving my husband.

Both kids went out to say hello and came back inside, having taken the few minutes Brad was willing to give them. They went upstairs to change into their pajamas, and Brad came inside.

"Where have you been?" he asked, and I couldn't tell if he was jolly drunk or jerk drunk.

"I took the kids out to dinner." I straightened the papers and mail strewn across the island. Brad sat down with his beer on the other side of the counter from me. "How was work?"

"Brutal." He took a long sip of his beer and watched me as I sprayed cleaner on the counter and wiped it down.

I ran my hand over the glistening quartz, and the memory of the colonel's lips between my legs shot through me. I lowered my face, hiding from my husband, as the vivid memories from a dream washed over me. The colonel's hands on my breasts as his tongue sent an orgasm through my body that nearly tore me in half. *If you are a whore, you're my whore.*

"My counterpart in London should suck my dick."

"Oh," was all I could muster. "I'll be right back." I forced myself to walk to the bathroom and stared at my reflection in the mirror searching for answers. He'd said, "If you are a whore, you're my whore." He'd said that. I hadn't dreamed it, or had I? I splashed water on my face and straightened my shirt.

I'd only had sex in my mind.

"Maybe we should go to church," I said when I returned to the kitchen.

"That's funny. I was just thinking we should go to bed and you could give me a blow job. Crazy how we're on the same page."

"I'm serious."

"So am I," Brad said.

I avoided Brad the rest of the night. I didn't want to have sex with him. I wasn't impressed with his early return. Before nine P.M. on a Friday night, he was nothing more than an interruption in the kids and my life. He drank too much, turned the television to whatever channel he wished, and expected me to ride him while he watched game two of the World Series.

When he came to bed smelling of beer and less than coordinated, he mounted me and fucked me until he came. He barely finished before he passed out.

Yes. We needed to go to church.

twenty-two

THERE WERE FEW THINGS WORSE than moving. Not a root canal. Not rain on your vacation. Not childbirth. It would have to be something painful and consuming with no definitive end to compare it to. Like a tax audit or a divorce.

To my complete surprise, I'd been able to convince Brad our family belonged in the house that began as a tavern. He was after all, my favorite drunk. It had taken less effort than I'd expected, and Brad really seemed to be putting me before his own needs and desires. It was foreign in our relationship, but I wasn't going to argue with him. He was eventually going to love the house.

I'd spent weeks going through items we needed to get rid of instead of move to the house, and it still didn't make our current house look any more appealing. The basement was slightly emptier, which Brad kept telling me would benefit us when we moved, but it did little for the aesthetics of the house. One thing I never complained about in the house was its storage space, but after spending hours cleaning and organizing, even that was working against me.

As I pulled everything from my bathroom vanity, I put the items into three piles: need now, need in new house, never needed in the first place. The steam jewelry cleaner Brad's mother had bought me as a wedding shower present went into the third pile. I had three open boxes of tampons. When I consolidated the boxes, I found a wad of cash in the bottom of the third.

The sick truth of nefarious intentions seeped into my mind. Why would a housewife have cash hidden? The purse I'd lied to Brad about came to mind and was followed by another thought. I was planning on running away, which made no sense. I would never leave Liv and James here alone. I would never leave them anywhere.

I counted the money. Six hundred dollars. That was a lot of secrets, or just one really big one.

Why can't I remember?

I put my head in my hands and squeezed it, willing the memories to be set free. Brad's desperation at the shore when he'd *needed* to make love to me and his kindness and willingness to sell the house, were the only things that came back.

I was afraid of him.

Even without the memories, I knew I was afraid of him, which was ridiculous. In the decade I'd known him, I'd never been afraid of him once. I'd been overwhelmed a few times, but never afraid. He was Brad. He was my husband.

I heard the door to the kitchen close downstairs and re-stashed the money in the tampon box. Yes. I smiled at my former self for selecting the hiding place. Brad would never open the box.

I'D CHECKED THEIR COSTUMES IN their backpacks twice to make sure all the parts were in there. This was the first year since I'd quit the Department of Justice that I wasn't working one of my kid's Halloween parties at school. The first time I was working myself. The colonel, Thompson, whose granddaughter was in the elementary school, and I were all going to drive over together. What a difference a year made.

I had on a black dress and the creepiest eyeball necklace I could find. Like, an entire eyeball hung from the chain around my neck.

"That is disgusting," Daniels said when he saw it.

"It's Halloween. Are you dressing up?"

"No."

"Well, it sounds like you're no fun."

"Oh, I'm fun. Tons of fun. That's what the ladies call me, Fun Daniels." Daniels was enormous. He was over six feet tall and almost as wide. He was a giant muscle, undeniably attractive, and overly confident. He was young.

"I stand corrected."

The colonel and Thompson stopped at my desk. I grabbed my bag and phone and followed them out the door, which the colonel held for me. As soon as I got in the back of the patrol car, my phone dinged with a text from Jenna.

Jenna: Where the hell are you?

It made me smile. Jenna always made me smile. I texted her back.

Meredith: On my way.

I dropped the phone on my lap and looked up to see the colonel watching me in the rearview mirror. Instead of turning away, I stared back.

"What are your kids this year?" Thompson asked the colonel, breaking his spell on me.

"Allison's a rabbit . . ."

I didn't listen to the rest. I couldn't hear him through the exploration of my mind, the search for any connection Vince might have to a wad of cash in the tampon box in my bathroom. Vince parked about a half mile away, because God forbid the entire town not come out for the elementary school parade.

"Are you going to be all right in those shoes? I can drop you off."

"I'll be fine. Thanks, though." I got out of the patrol car and shut the door behind me. There was a balmy breeze and a dark cloud above us that threatened to ruin the trick-or-treating later.

"Shit," Thompson said and stopped walking. The colonel stopped, too, and both of them stared down the street at a man three houses in front of us who was barely on his feet, tripping from the curb to the other side of the walk.

"Why does he do this?" the colonel said, and then turned to me. "You go ahead."

"What?"

"That's Arnie Hampton. Alex's dad."

The man in front of us was barely recognizable, but when we got closer, I could hear him muttering something.

"Goddamn her! Motherfucking whore gonna leave me. I'll show her," he said and almost fell over.

Thompson ran ahead and grabbed Arnie by the arm, helping to keep him on his feet.

Vince stopped me with a hand on my elbow, and heat shot through me. "Go ahead of us. And if we don't make it to the parade, call me and I'll send someone to pick you up."

I looked from his hand on my arm to Arnie again. The man was belligerent and pulling away from Thompson, who was trying to turn him around and lead him away from the school. "But you'll miss the parade?"

"That's better than Arnie not missing it. His poor kids."

Arnie turned to Thompson and spit on him, and then he was face down on the ground with his arm at Thompson's mercy.

"Go, please."

I did as he asked. I walked the rest of the way by myself, and I wondered how many times a day the colonel put someone else before himself and his own family.

"Took you long enough," Jenna said and rolled her eyes at me when I reached her on the parade route.

"I didn't miss Liv and James, did I?"

"No. Kindergarten just went by. You're good." Jenna had a coffee cup in her hand, and I wondered what was in it. She'd always had secrets. It was one of the reasons I loved her in the first place. It made me believe she could keep mine if I had any.

"Did you ever see me with a lot of cash?" I asked.

She stopped drinking and studied me. "What do you mean?"

"Did I ever seem to have a wad of cash on me or stashed someplace in my house?"

"No." She shook her head, confused. "You did have a bunch in your purse when we took the kids to the waterpark last year." The waterpark I couldn't remember.

"Did I say what it was for?"

"I think you said you were saving for Brad's Christmas present."

That made sense. I'd hide the cash in a place Brad would never look. I'd bought him a suitcase for Christmas. It could have been expensive. I should have felt better. It should have put my mind at ease, but it didn't. If I used the cash to buy the suitcase, what was in the tampon box? I couldn't stop thinking about the dead feeling I had around Brad.

"Was I ever . . . afraid? Of Brad?"

Jenna searched my eyes for the answer I wanted to hear, but what I needed was the truth. I trusted her to give it to me. "Why would you ask that?"

"Because I can't remember anything, and the things that are coming back are scaring me." My voice cracked on my last words. I was cracking.

"About Brad? Did he hurt you?" Jenna was winding up. She was moving past our conversation to a sheer anger at Brad.

"No. Not that I know of. Did I ever seem afraid of him?" I tried to diffuse her, but I still needed answers.

"No. I would have done something. I told you, you were a lot of things last year, but I didn't get the sense you were afraid."

I sighed and let the relief flow through me. This was crazy. I wasn't afraid of my husband. Brad would never hurt me.

"But you should ask your boss about it."

"What?" I asked without thinking.

"After you fell, the chief came to my house, asking questions about you and Brad. Did I think he could hurt you? How was your marriage?"

"He did?"

"He seemed to think Brad hurt you."

I knew the colonel had so many answers, but he wasn't telling me anything. And for some reason that I couldn't explain even to myself, I knew I shouldn't ask him.

"And he seemed pretty pissed off about it," she added. "So maybe he knew something."

"I'll ask him."

Liv walked by, and I jumped in front of the crowd and snapped a picture of her. She was a pregnant bowler. I thought it was inappropriate, but I couldn't find the words to convey why to her and she loved the idea. She wore saddle shoes, plaid pants, and a polo shirt with a pillow stuffed under the front of it. She carried a bowling ball made out of papier-mâché in her hand and smiled brightly with her seventies sunglasses on. She loved the eyeball necklace hanging from my neck.

James walked by and stopped his two friends so I could take a picture of all of them together. They were the see-no-evil, hear-no-evil, speak-no-evil monkeys. James was hear-no-evil, and I could tell his arms were getting tired. Liv had told him they would.

"Do you know where Vince is?" Lynn Pratt was standing next to me. I recognized her from the few parties we'd worked together at the school and from her wedding portrait in the colonel's office.

"He was here. There was a problem. He said he was going to try to make it back in time."

Lynn rolled her eyes. "Typical."

"He was a block away. I know he wanted to be here."

"I know." She softened. "Are you headed back there?"

"Actually, I need a ride. I came with him and Thompson." I searched the crowd for Jenna.

"I can drop you off. It's right on my way," Lynn offered, and my instincts told me to say no, but to do so would have been obvious of some discomfort in her presence that wasn't even obvious to me . . . yet.

Lynn smiled, and we walked to her car, easily making conversation about Liv and Allison and their Halloween costumes. She seemed to have a much higher tolerance for Liv's costume than some of the other mothers did. I loved her for it.

When we were locked inside her car, with our seatbelts on and the windows up, Lynn asked, "How does he seem?"

"The chief?" I asked, knowing exactly who she meant but not willing to talk about him to his wife.

"Do you know?"

I didn't know what to say. The colonel would know, but I was alone and I didn't want to hurt her any more than I wanted to hurt him. "Only because I stupidly asked him if you guys might be interested in buying my house. Brad and I are moving."

"What did he say?"

"That you two had separated."

"Did he say why?" she asked. She was pushing, and I could sense her desperation, but I couldn't help her. She knew her husband better than I did.

"He didn't. He didn't say much at all, but we're not that close." I scrunched up my face, mirroring the awkwardness of this conversation.

"He's always had a great deal of respect for you. I thought

he might have." Lynn was lost in her own words. They trailed off as if replaced by other thoughts before she could even speak them. She was talking to me, but her mind was a million miles away.

"I don't think he'll tell anyone something he hasn't told you." I peered out the windshield. The colonel was a gentlemen. He wouldn't speak out of turn about his wife or his marriage.

"I know this is putting you in a bad spot." I braced myself and cursed myself for accepting the ride. "But has he seen anyone or has anyone called him?" I turned to Lynn, who was intently watching the road, not facing me on purpose. "A woman," she said, finally showing her hand.

"Not a soul. I swear." It was at that moment I realized the colonel had left his wife, not the other way around. He'd left her with nothing but questions.

Lynn stopped her car at the back door of the station and made no move to get out.

"Thanks for the ride," I said and collected my bag. "I hope things work out." I didn't offer to help. I didn't tell her "anything you need," because I couldn't. Not only did I work with her husband but also I dreamed of him, too.

twenty-three

SOMETIMES I DREAMED OF BRAD, but many of those were nightmares. He was yelling at me. He was chasing me. He was angry. The last one was the only one of the three that I saw while I was awake. I needed some perspective in order to sort everything out. The fragments my mind released, combined with the dreams and the things I found around my house, were driving me to the brink of insanity.

With no other ideas of how to reconcile everything going on in my head, I took my family to church. Since it wasn't Scout Sunday, both of our children were signed into Sunday school, and Brad and I could relax during the service. We sat a few rows from the front. Brad put his arm around my shoulders. It was cold in the church, and I leaned toward him, seeking some heat.

The colonel and Lynn came in with their oldest son. They sat directly in front of us, their son between them. I smiled to Lynn when she turned around before she sat down. It was the kind of tiny gesture women gave each other when their kids were melting down in Target. It said, "I'm sorry," without saying another word because we knew the other woman didn't want to hear our shit, or anyone else's.

The colonel rested his arm on the back of his son's chair in front of me, and I studied the cuff of his shirt. The sight of him buttoning it and his bare chest from the day I'd walked in on him half dressed in his office played again in my mind and warmed me. His hand was large and tan, like the rest of him. His wedding ring was silver and still at home on the fourth finger of his left hand. He was married.

I was married.

The congregation stood and prayed together. When we finished The Lord's Prayer, I added my own.

Dear God, Please let me stop dreaming about the colonel. Let me love my husband. Let me live the life I have and be happy.

When I opened my eyes, Brad was staring at me. More like inspecting me. He would ask me later what I was praying for. He would want to know what I found so important that I would talk to God about it, and I would lie.

The pastor talked about family, support, and character. He cited the Book of Daniel from the Old Testament and the lion's den. The colonel squeezed his son's shoulder and looked across at Lynn. The Pratts were exceptional. To the outsider, there was no contempt, no hatred. They were a united team with their child between them, solidifying one more support system for their torn family.

My brother, Pink Floyd, and a giant bag of weed had been my support system when my parents had split. We'd never gone to church. I'd never seen my parents smile at each other after my father had moved out. They barely could speak to each other to arrange a ride for the two of us. Their relationship had been toxic.

Brad shifted in his seat. He took back his arm and checked the time on his watch. He'd had enough of Daniel. I'd barely heard a word. How could I understand words and concepts with the sweet smell of mahogany so close? I lowered my head and inhaled slowly. There was a way to release myself from the hold the colonel had on me, but apparently, it wasn't with God. *Figures.*

The sermon ended, and Liv and James ran into the sanctuary, excited to share everything they'd learned in Sunday school.

They each grabbed a cookie from the table in the back and endured Brad's complaints about them eating in his car.

As soon as we were all buckled in I said, "Okay, so tell me what you learned in Sunday school." Brad watched for pedestrians and pulled onto the road without listening to a word the kids and I were saying.

"We learned about Daniel and the lion's den," James said.

"So did we," Liv added. She was in a different class than James.

"So did we," I chimed in, and James was thrilled we were all on the same page. "What specifically did you learn?"

James thought for a minute. "That our character has consequences."

"Oh. Interesting. Do you know what our character is?"

"It's what we believe in," Liv said, and James turned to her, mad she was butting in on his explanation.

"It's not just what we believe. It's the things we do and say because of what we believe."

"Whatever." Liv was done with the conversation. She stared out the window and sang the wrong words to a pop song that would now be stuck in my head for a week.

"So how does our character have consequences?" I asked, trying to appease James.

"If you're honest, people will trust you," James said.

"Oh, I like that. I want you both to be honest." I turned in my seat and looked both of my children in the eyes to solidify my point.

"And the consequence for lying is punishment." James was so severe with the statement. Although, he'd just spent an hour learning about Daniel being thrown into an actual lion's den to be eaten throughout the night. Not much of the Bible was sugarcoated.

Brad shifted in his seat. He'd been sitting too long. He was uncomfortable.

Liv stopped singing and added, "My teacher told us sin is like a disease. When we sin, it's passed on to others. It doesn't ever just affect us." She sat back in her seat, satisfied with her contribution. "Oh, and she said, 'we have to be disciplined,' but I didn't know what that meant."

"You should ask if you're not sure what something means," I told her.

"I was busy making a cross out of yarn and Popsicle sticks." She held up a neon-colored cross and smiled as if crafts were the real point of church.

"It's beautiful," I said, not meaning it.

"It's awesome," Liv corrected me. "I feel bad there are so many families in the world without an Olivia."

I turned around in my seat as Brad took out his phone, swiped the screen, and read something. All while he drove his entire family home from church.

"Is that an emergency?" We were less than a mile from our house.

Brad glared at his phone, periodically glancing at the road as if it were the nuisance. His anxiousness about sitting too long was replaced by irritation. "It's work," he said, and any serenity church had instilled in me was immediately replaced by a cold bitterness toward my husband. Two words. That was all it took.

"Sorry." I stared out the window. I missed *not* feeling utter disappointment in the man I'd married.

Brad pulled the car into his garage bay, and the kids ran into the house, happy to finally be some place they were free to yell and run around. Brad finished reading his phone, shut it off, and leaned up to slide it back in his pants pocket. "I've got to go into the office for a while."

"On a Sunday?"

"Meredith, I work. Things come up. Even you should be

able to remember what it was like to have responsibilities."

The words stung me. I sat completely still and let contempt and resentment fill me.

Brad got out of the car and went into the house, and I sat in the garage alone. He wasn't abusive. His words weren't even that cruel. But he hurt me. Almost everything he did hurt me in some way.

Six hundred dollars in cash made more sense. But it was nothing. If I'd actually thought about leaving my husband, six hundred dollars wasn't going to get me very far. It wouldn't even get me a few hours at an attorney's office.

There was something else. There had to be.

twenty-four

IT WAS THE END OF November, and the weeks had flown by with me working at the police station four days a week and dreaming of the colonel every night. The dreams grew more frequent and more intense with each moment I spent in his presence. The days were excruciating as the memories of the night before came back, and my own memories stayed silent in my mind. I needed help, but I didn't know who to turn to for it.

"Have you ever dreamed of having sex with another man?" I asked Jenna with a light tone. It wasn't a big deal. Just some dream sex. I sat next to her on my back porch as the kids ran around my yard, playing manhunt.

"Probably. I don't know." Jenna took a drag of her cigarette. "Who are you dreaming about?" She sat up and faced me with a huge grin. "And don't try to tell me no one."

"I've had dreams about my boss."

"Dreamssss? As in more than one?" she asked, suddenly full of energy.

"No. Just one." I shook my head and added, "Every night. Just one a night."

She slapped me across the shoulder. "Tell!"

The kids all stopped running to see why they were being yelled at.

"False alarm," Jenna yelled into the group, and they returned to their search-and-rescue operation. She turned back to me. "When you say boss, are you talking about the chief?"

I should have regretted telling her, but I didn't. It was such a relief having someone to talk to about it. Maybe they'd stop if I talked about them. Maybe exposing them to the light would silence them. "Yes. Vincent Pratt." I stood, frozen in my spot, and scrutinized Jenna's reaction, but she was only doing the same to me. "What do you think that means?"

"Like, what kind of dreams are we talking about? Holding hands? Kissing?" She was calming down, settling into the thought that this was innocent.

"Last night, I dreamed he was fucking me on top of his police cruiser, and I swear I had an orgasm in my sleep." Jenna's mouth fell open. She was blinking and making me uncomfortable. "It's not normal, is it?"

"Do you like him? You know he and his wife split up, right? Does he flirt with you?"

"No. Yes." I shook my head. "No. He's always the perfect gentleman around me." It was impossible to hide the disappointment in my voice.

"Okay, let's back up. You've been having dreams about your boss every night for how long?"

I thought back as far as I could remember. "Since right after I hurt my head." Tears filled my eyes. I wasn't sure what part was upsetting me. Not knowing if I'd had sex dreams about him before August, or the fact that I was having them now. "It's crazy."

"Aw, it's not so crazy. You spend more time with him than you do your husband, and he's hot. If you're into the cop thing. I'm guessing he doesn't get high."

I laughed at her and her priorities. "I'm guessing not, but I haven't asked him."

"Maybe you should tell him you dream about him. Maybe he dreams about you, too."

"And then what? We can exchange notes on how he

handcuffed me in a hotel in Philadelphia?"

"You dreamed that, too?" Gaping mouth again. "What the fuck? I need to get a job at the police station."

"I would love that," I said as the sun completely disappeared behind the trees.

"Is Brad going to be home in time for Thanksgiving?"

"He says he is. He's supposed to land Tuesday night, late."

"Maybe if he were in town a little more, you'd stop dreaming about the chief."

I sighed. "Maybe."

THAT NIGHT I DREAMED THE colonel and I were swimming in the ocean. We were floating out past the breakers, and he promised me I wasn't a whore. But I already knew I wasn't because he was in love with me, and he was too good to love a whore. I kissed him, and he told me he loved me, but then a rip current pulled him away. No matter how fast I swam, I couldn't catch up to him. He kept moving farther and farther away.

I woke up alone in my bed and alone in my mind. I wanted to call him, and for some reason that I couldn't remember, I had his number. I yearned for him to touch me the way he did in my dreams. I wanted him to hold me as I buried my face in his chest and forgot that which I'd forgotten. But I rolled over and lay by myself until the sun came up.

twenty-five

I DROVE HOME FROM MY brother's on Thanksgiving. It was only seven thirty, but the sun had set hours before. It was twenty-six degrees out, and Brad adjusted the heat in the car until I almost died of suffocation and had to turn it down. He'd drunk too much at dinner and then drank some more while the rest of the adults had cleaned up. I was hoping he'd pass out, but he stayed awake reading something on his phone.

"I'm going to stop at the station on the way home," I said. "I made some brownies for the guys on duty."

"No." It wasn't even a question. Just a definitive no. I hated him for thinking he was in control of me.

"Why? It'll just take a second."

"I'm tired. I'm jet lagged. I need to go home."

"You're thirsty." I rolled my eyes. "You should have brought a beer with you for the ride."

"Drop me off at the house before you go to the station." Brad shifted in his seat. He was tired of sitting while I drove his ass home. "Or just stay home with me and take them in when you go in next week."

"They're a thank you for working on a national holiday. I'm not taking them five days later."

Brad shut up and closed his eyes, but when a song I liked came on the radio, he managed to move just enough to change the station. He was a treat.

ONCE BRAD WAS COMFORTABLE AND the kids were in bed, I grabbed my brownies and headed out the door. It was silly. They weren't even all that special, the double chocolate box type Liv helped me make the day before.

I pulled into the station and ignored my disappointment at the absence of the colonel's truck. He wasn't there. He couldn't be here twenty-four hours a day. I carried the brownies into the barracks and faced my empty desk and the colonel's empty office. It wasn't the same without him.

"Meredith, did you miss me?" Daniels flew around the corner and took the brownies from my hands. "Oh, you *did* miss me." He reached under the wrapping and grabbed a brownie. I watched as he put the entire thing in his mouth and closed his eyes while he chewed. He was barely an adult, and unbelievably a police officer.

"Happy Thanksgiving, Officer Daniels."

"You, too," he said and kissed me on the cheek. It was a kiss your neighbors and friends' husbands would give—warm and full of heart.

"Who's here with you?" I asked, not used to Officer Daniel's tender side.

"Thompson, Collins, and Tencza are out on patrol. The chief left about an hour ago."

"Did you get to have dinner?"

"Oh, hell yeah. I'm not missing stuffing, mashed potatoes, and turkey for anyone. The chief missed out on the whole day, though."

I put the plate of brownies on the counter in the break room, separated four onto a different plate, and wrapped them with foil from the drawer. The rest I left for the other officers with a note saying "Happy Thanksgiving." I waved to Daniels and headed out the door.

My car was already cold again, and it didn't heat up on the three-minute drive to the house the colonel was living in. If you could call living in a demolition zone living. I parked far back in the driveway. I didn't want anyone to see my car here, but I didn't know why. I could visit him. There was nothing to hide. I would even tell Brad when I got home if he was still conscious.

I hopped out of the Escalade and pulled my coat around my ears. I could see the colonel through the cracked window of the door. He was painting in the back room of the house, wearing sweatpants that hung low and no shirt. The muscles in his back flexed as he reached to the top of the wall. I realized I was breathing heavy when my breath fogged the window. I closed my eyes and welcomed the silent recount of my dreams where he was throbbing and pushing inside of me. This wasn't normal. *This* wasn't me. I forced the thoughts from my mind. I was here to show my gratitude. It was an innocent gesture, but the way my nipples hardened at the sight of him didn't feel innocent.

I opened the screen door and knocked on the wooden one, but the colonel never came. I knocked again, but he still didn't answer. With my ear to the door, I could hear a radio playing inside the house. I turned the knob and opened the door, just leaning in, leaving my feet still outside until I'd been invited. "Hello," I said toward the radio. The colonel wasn't in sight. "Hello," I said, louder this time, and he stuck his head out around the corner.

"What are you doing here?" he asked, looking around for a place to put down his paintbrush. He rested it on a can top in the corner of the room and rushed over to me. "Come in. It's freezing out."

I stepped into the house and closed the door behind me. My sight skipped to his chest and then I forced it away. I looked around the room to avoid staring, which was exactly what I wanted to do. The heat in the house was almost unbearable.

I unzipped my parka and took it off without being invited to.

"It's so warm in here," I said, and my chest heaved. My longing for him rested across the center of it, making it hard to breathe. It was a mistake to have come. A recap of the Cowboys game blared in the background.

The colonel turned down the volume on the radio and faced me again. "The radiators have only one setting: hot as hell." He laughed, and I watched his body move and tried to think.

The heat traveled from my breasts to my throat, and I swallowed it down, wanting him. I needed to concentrate on something other than his body. "I brought you some brownies." I extended the plate to him. "Happy Thanksgiving."

"Oh." He took the plate and lifted the foil. "You didn't have to do that."

"I figured your first Thanksgiving alone might be a tough one."

The colonel held the brownies in his hands, and my heart with his eyes. He wouldn't release it. He stared at me until a tiny smile settled on his mouth, and I feared the small gesture might break me.

"Come here." He nodded toward the kitchen. "You can help me with something." I followed him into the kitchen, happy to be away from the door. The floor was covered in drop cloths, a painting light beamed bright over the entire room, and a cardboard table was set up in the far corner. He handed me two squares of granite and said, "The cabinets are going to be dark wood. Very traditional. I can't decide on a countertop."

I turned the granite in my hands, looking at them from every direction.

"When do you move?" he asked, and stole my attention from the stones.

"We settle—well, I'm *closing* on the house December thirtieth. Brad is settling that day." The colonel and I both laughed at poor Brad. "He'll come around."

"What if he doesn't?" he asked, and I stopped laughing.

I returned to the safety of the granite in my hands and said, "This one." I handed him the sand-colored sample. "It looks like the wet sand after the tide has gone out."

"I knew you were going to say that."

He was standing next to me, but he may as well have been on top of me. His shoulder was so close to my face the smell of his skin was choking the words in my throat. I relived what it felt like the day I'd walked in on him in his office without his shirt on. I was suddenly terrified to remember more.

"How did you know I would say that?" My head turned slowly, and my body followed until I was standing only inches away, facing him. Trying to face *this*. Whatever this was.

I could have kissed him. I ached to taste him to the point of anger. The desire rose up inside of me and burned through the image of his sweet face, leaving nothing but outrage in its place. The colonel leaned toward me, and I needed his lips on mine. I forced my eyes closed to hide from that which I wanted more than air.

"What are you thinking? Tell me the truth," he pleaded, and I knew it wasn't the first time he'd demanded honesty from me.

I was flushed, and my emotions were overwrought. But I forced myself to look him in the eyes when I said, "I've lost almost an entire year, and the things that keep appearing in my mind, make me believe I don't know myself anymore."

"Like what?"

"Like wanting you to kiss me right now." I wouldn't turn away. "Regardless of the cost." The physical pain of coveting him centered behind my eyes. "But that's not who I am."

Vince lowered his head. He groaned as he shook it. I waited. I stayed perfectly still, bracing myself for the truth he would share. "I just want you to be safe and happy."

Those were the only words he said. He wasn't going to tell me anything. And for some reason, I trusted him more than my husband who'd told me everything. I sensed the truth might hurt me more than the unknown, but it did nothing to quell the unknown inside me.

twenty-six

I TRIED TO STAY AWAY from him. I tried not to inhale him like a dog as he walked by. I even tried to tell myself he was ugly. Disgusting, actually. He wasn't as amazing as he was in my head. Surely, he had tons of faults, and his thick black hair and the width of his chest were blinding me to them.

This was how I started each day, and by the end of each one, I was still in love with him. If he smiled or didn't. If he spoke to me or not. None of it mattered. I just wanted to be near him. I knew, without a doubt, I had to quit my job. I couldn't stay here fawning over him every day. Nothing good could come of it. But, I didn't think I could leave—him or my desk.

My cell phone ringing startled me. I knew Brad was going to call, but the sound still broke through my daily activity of imagining what the colonel looked like when he slept.

"Hello," I said as I slid the green icon on my phone to the side.

"I'm here. Can we go get this over with?"

The smile drained from my face. Brad didn't want to close on our new house. He didn't want the house at all, and he was going to make me pay for it by complaining every step of the way. I considered just hanging up and not going outside. Letting the settlement pass and staying in the house he loved, but I loved the new house more than I loved Brad.

Deep breath.

"Do you have to be this way?" My voice was low, barely above a whisper.

The colonel and Thompson were studying a map hanging four feet from my desk.

"Yes! I have to fucking be this way. Now can you come out of the fucking police station so we can buy this fucking disgusting house?"

The colonel and Thompson turned to me, able to hear every word through my cell. My cheeks flushed. I was mortified by how my husband had spoken to me, and I could have killed him for it.

I hung up the phone and smiled at the officers. "I have to go. Today is settlement," I said to them.

They were still staring at me in shock. Neither of them would ever speak to me that way. Until recently, neither would my husband.

"Everything okay? How about I walk you out?"

Vince thinks Brad hurt me.

"His bark is worse than his bite. I'll be fine."

"Are you coming back?"

"Not until tomorrow."

"Text me later and let me know you're all right."

I stared at him. I wanted to stay here with him. "I will."

"Don't forget, or I'm coming to your house."

I was the only one who smiled. The colonel meant it, and Thompson knew he'd do it.

"I won't forget," I said and held the colonel's eyes a little too long. I'd forgotten just about everything else.

Brad was waiting in his black sedan with all the windows up and the music blaring. He was a child. I opened the door, and he didn't even turn to me. I leaned in and shut off the stereo.

"I'll drive myself," I said and moved back from the center of the car.

"Why?" For a second, I thought he was drunk, but he was

wound too tight. He was just a giant dick.

"Because you seem a bit agitated, so I'd rather ride alone than be near you."

"That's nice, Meredith."

"Well what do you expect? Why are you screaming curse words at me because we're buying a house? One that you helped pick out?"

He glared through the front windshield again, and I slammed the passenger door and stormed toward the Escalade. I heard his driver's door slam behind me, and then he was in front of me.

"Don't be an asshole," he said.

Takes. One. To. Know. One.

"What is your problem? You yell at the kids. You yell at me. You don't talk anymore. What the hell is going on with you?"

"I work!" he exploded. His arms flew up in the air, and the blood rushed to his face. I took a step back, out of his reach, and even that pissed him off. "What, are you afraid of me now?"

"No." There was a moment of silence, and in it, I felt the fear of my husband return. I wasn't afraid he'd hurt me. I was afraid of what he would take from me. "If this is really about the house, I don't want it." Brad's jaw loosened and his hands relaxed at his sides. "It's not worth this much to me."

"How much, Meredith? How much is it worth?" He wasn't making any sense.

"What are you talking about?"

Brad roughly ran his hand through his hair. He was losing his grip. Without his anger, he was lost in this conversation. "Nothing. Ride with me." He grabbed my arm, and I pulled it away at the exact moment the back door of the police station opened and the colonel stepped out. He stood near the door, his eyes fixed on me and Brad's eyes fixed on him.

"Let's go. I'll ride with you," I said, and Brad turned toward me. Relief crossed his face for the first time since I'd walked into the parking lot.

We walked back to his car under the rage of the colonel's stare. When I was safely in the passenger seat with the door shut, I looked at him and smiled.

I knew I had to quit my job.

twenty-seven

BRAD AND I SETTLED, BUT made no mention of moving into our new house. Instead, we hired a contractor to renovate the kitchen and baths and raise the ceiling in the master bedroom. I swore to Brad that he'd love it when the work was done. We also hired a landscaper to build us a backyard worthy of my husband's approval, and I promised to have a party in the spring. I'd do anything for him to love the house.

Despite all of that, Brad was still angry all the time.

"Can we talk about the pros and cons of having two heads?" James asked, causing Brad to look at me. He wanted reassurance these weren't his children. He was hoping this was the moment I'd confess they belonged to someone else. "The major pro is you're twice as smart," James continued without caring if anyone was listening. "The con is if you have a fight with your other head, you can only control half your body."

"Can we talk about you chewing with your mouth shut?" Brad asked, and it was a valid question. I was constantly reminding James about his table manners, but the way Brad said it was cruel. As if James should stop because it disgusted him rather than a father's desire for his son to be the best he could be.

James finished his food and asked to be excused without another word.

After the kids left the kitchen and I'd cleaned up breakfast, I asked Brad the question he always refused to answer. "Is everything okay with you?"

"Fine. Why do you ask?"

I needed to tread lightly. The last few times I'd asked had ended with Brad blowing up at me or the children. "Because I love you." What could there be to argue about that? I cared because I loved him.

"I'm sorry. There's just a lot going on at work that's stressing me. I haven't been sleeping well. I don't know . . ."

"Is it the house?" The guilt for making him buy it returned.

"No. The house is fine. I want you to be happy."

"I'm thinking about quitting my job," I blurted out without completely thinking it through. I knew I needed to quit, I just didn't think that I ever would.

Brad's face lit up the same way it did when I'd accepted his wedding proposal. My sight fell to the blue topaz ring on my finger. He was meant for me. The ring proved it. He'd known I wouldn't want a diamond. He knew me better than anyone else did. "I would love it if you quit your job."

"Has it been that much of an inconvenience?"

"No, no." Brad pulled me close to him and wrapped his arms around my back. "I'd just like to keep you all to myself." I rested my face against his chest and listened to his heartbeat. It was racing against my cheek. I could feel the ugly sense of loss settling in my soul. The job was the only thing that was mine. And now I'd give it up for Brad to be happy.

❧

I WAS MAKING MYSELF A cup of tea when the colonel walked into the break room. I kept my face down and inhaled deeply as he reached across me for sugar.

"Pardon me," he said close to my ear. His voice was soft. I dunked my teabag in my cup, and remembered crying when he left my house in the middle of the night. He was standing in my kitchen, and James was yelling my name from his bedroom. The colonel had walked out the back door, and I'd thought I'd fall to the floor and never stand again. "Meredith?"

I was sure my face told him the whole story. He'd left me. At some point in the year before, he'd left me crying in my kitchen, and that had everything to do with why he wasn't telling me the truth about us now.

"Do you have a few minutes we could speak . . . privately?" I asked and stepped away from him. The empty feeling seeped behind my chest and rose to my throat. I didn't want to be without him, in my memory or now.

"Of course. Come in my office."

I followed him in. I sat down in the chair and the memory of a time I was in the chair before startled me. I was angry with him. He'd given Jenna a DUI after her accident, and I'd come here to scream at him.

"I remembered some things."

The colonel stayed silent. He sat behind his desk like any normal boss would.

"The only memories that come back to me are about you." My inspection covered his office, seeking every detail my mind would release. My sight landed on his wedding picture. It was facing me from the credenza to the side of his desk. He and Lynn barely looked old enough to drink in it.

"What did you remember?" He pulled me back to him.

"Nothing you don't already know about." My voice didn't sound like my own. It was deep, harboring the darkness of the memory of him leaving. I wanted to curl up in my bed and lay there silent with my knees to my chest. "I'm going to have to quit my job here."

"What?" He was on his feet and circling the desk before I reacted to his question. "Why? Because your husband is making you?"

I couldn't find the words. I wasn't sure exactly why, only that if I was going to save my marriage, I had to. "No."

"Then why? You love it here." The colonel moved the chair from the corner of the room next to mine and sat down. "And we love having you here."

"I think it's wrong for me to be here." He leaned back and pondered me. It wasn't fair how much he knew about me. About us. "You seem determined to let me remember everything on my own. I don't know why, but I trust you enough to know it's not good. Or maybe we weren't good."

"It's not like that."

"What is it like then? Tell me everything you know," I pleaded with him.

"Your memory is coming back. More and more each day. If it comes from me, it won't give you any more solace than you have now. You won't know whether to believe me. I need it to come from you." His eyes mirrored the anguish I felt. The colonel knew what it was like to lose me too, he was the one who'd walked out, and now he needed me to come back on my own.

The way I'd hungered for him on Thanksgiving night returned and solidified what I already knew. "It's not right for me to come here every day." I didn't elaborate. I couldn't without getting into the dreams that still haunted me. The ones where he touched me. The ones where I cried out and came with his hands on me.

"I know you don't owe me anything, but do this one thing for me," he said, taking my hand in his. The warmth spread through me like a drug, and I couldn't take my eyes off his fingers around my own. "Stay working here until your memory fully returns." My head shook without me telling it to. "I won't sleep. I'll worry about you every day. Just keep the job until you remember, and then, if you want to leave, you don't even have to give me two weeks' notice. You can stop the minute you're ready to."

"You think he'll hurt me," I said, or maybe asked. I watched for the colonel's expression to change, but he stayed still. "Or you think he already did."

The statement broke him, and he tightened his grip on my hand. "Only you and he know what happened that day, but I need to know before you quit this job."

"What if I never remember?"

"You will."

I took back my hand and walked out of his office.

twenty-eight

I FINISHED WRAPPING THEIR GIFTS. Pink snowman paper for Liv, and silver toy soldiers for James. I'd had to convince Brad to take them to the children's holiday party at his office to get a few hours alone to finish. I'd told him it would humanize him among his employees who probably hated him as much as they respected him.

I found every scrap of paper on the floor, balled them together, and put them in the trash. I took the bag out to the can in the garage. It might be the last year Liv believed in Santa Claus, and I was determined to hold on to it as long as I could.

I stacked the presents in thick black lawn bags and carried them to the trunk of my car. Later, I'd drive them over and hide them in the new house. I'd spent every waking moment avoiding the colonel in my mind. I locked him out and replaced him with Liv, James, and my husband.

I went to church. I prayed Brad and I could survive this . . . That I could survive this. I wouldn't let the memories from Thanksgiving and my own dreams own me. It was a battle I lost every night. I dreamed of him. I wanted him, and nothing I did while I was awake could protect my marriage from the way I felt about him.

I put the tape and the scissors back in my desk and looked around, satisfied with the clean-up job. The door to the garage opened, and the house came back to life.

"Mommy!" Liv yelled.

James was the first to see me. He took off his coat and shoes and ran over to hug me. Liv wiggled her way in between us and with the two of them hugging me, we almost fell to the floor. Brad followed with a tote bag with his company's logo on the front. Liv grabbed it from him and started setting up the crafts she'd made at the party as a display for me. She then proceeded to show me the water bottles, pens, styluses, light-up keychains, and bottle openers they'd received as gifts.

"This is an odd children's gift," I said and held up the bottle opener.

"It's fun for the whole family," Brad responded and kissed me on the cheek. Liv sat, stoned-faced, watching Brad as he poured himself a glass of water. "I've got some work to do," he said and disappeared into his office, leaving me alone with my children and their cotton ball snow crafts.

"So. Tell me everything. How was it?" I asked James and Liv at the same time.

"It was good," James said, and I knew that was the whole story I'd get from him. He slipped out of the room as soon as Liv launched into every detail about the event. She was animated, and excited, and shared every minute from the car ride over the bridge to Philadelphia to the elevator ride in the parking garage when the party was over. But I never heard a word to explain why she'd glared at Brad the way she did when he'd kissed me.

I poured her a glass of milk and waited. I didn't say a word. I just lovingly smiled at her while she took a sip. She was dressed in a turtleneck and faux leather leggings. She'd looked so grown up as I'd braided the sides of her hair and clipped them behind her head that morning. Liv and James had promised Brad they'd act "normal." A word with a fluid definition in our house.

"Do you know a lot of Daddy's friends?" Liv finally asked,

and I kept the nonchalant, milk-drinking ease in my voice.

"Let's see. I know Amit. He's Daddy's best friend at the office. You would call him Mr. Jogal. Did you meet him?"

"Yes. He was nice." She took another sip of her milk, and I stayed silent. I could have filled the time. I could have let her off the hook, but I needed to know what was bothering her. Her sad little eyes would keep me awake for days. I didn't turn away and fill the dishwasher. I let whatever it was linger between us. "Have you ever met Daddy's friend Dharma?" Liv finally asked.

I kept still, smiling the whole time and hanging on her every tormented word. "I don't think I have. Is she nice? Did you like her?"

Liv stared at me, and I didn't know what to do, what she needed from me. She glanced back into the hallway and lowered her voice. It was so slight that if I weren't glued to her every word, I might not have noticed. She finally said, "When she laughs, she only looks at Daddy," and stared down into her glass of milk. Such a tremendous burden for a little girl. One who saw more than most adults.

She'd handed the weight to me, and it dragged me under the surface of my marriage. Brad was seeing someone, or at the very least, this woman wanted him to. I'd been lying to myself for so long, I'd started to believe my own version of my fairy tale, but the reality was far away from the storyline.

I held her hand and pulled it up to my mouth to kiss it. "I love you, Liv."

"I know," she said and finished her milk.

twenty-nine

THE HOLIDAYS CAME AND WENT. It was the last Christmas we spent in the house that I was now referring to as the "big house" because it felt like a prison to me. Brad took the time between Christmas Eve and New Year's off. He helped assemble the kids' toys and watched Christmas movies with us. He drank hot chocolate, he built a snowman, and he opened a bottle of wine for me every night. It was a cozy time. I told myself that whatever Liv had picked up on at the office party was misread. Brad was clearly not having an affair.

But then he went back to work, and I returned to being a single mother. The loneliness set back in. At least I had Jenna. She was my partner, and my favorite member of my team. Of the few words Brad had spoken to me and the kids in the weeks that followed his holiday vacation, none were kind. They were filled with frustration, anxiety, and resentment. I assumed it had something to do with his friend from the office, Dharma. The kids instinctively kept their distance from him. I could barely stand the sight of him.

"IF I'M NOT DRINKING, I'M going to need some ice cream to survive this," Jenna said as she hopped out of her car in the Latteria parking lot.

"Are you sure you're up to this?"

"Sobriety? Or this sleepover?" She laughed as she held the door open and our five kids rushed past us to the counter. We followed them in. I'd never been there, not that I remembered anyway. Jenna and I scanned the chalkboard for the flavors: Sweet Caramel Butterscotch, Banana Crunch, Chocolate Peanut Butter Swirl . . . sweet Jesus.

The kids all spoke at once, and somehow, the woman behind the counter got all their orders.

"Are you sure you're okay with them all sleeping at your house tonight?"

"Only if you're going to be okay the night they all sleep at yours." Jenna laughed a devious laugh, and I knew she'd hold me to it. This was a huge waste, since Brad was out of town, but I could use the time to continue the never-ending packing. "What are you getting?"

"I'm not sure. Nothing with nuts," I said, and almost knocked myself over with the words. They weren't mine. The colonel had said them to me.

"Since when don't you like nuts?"

"I don't know." I held on to the countertop as "Bourbon Cookies and Cream" came out of my mouth. "A large, please." I let the sight of our children eating their ice cream mesmerize me, and I paid for our order. It was the least I could do. The woman behind the counter smiled at me like she knew me, but I was getting used to that. Lots of people hinted at things I no longer knew anything about. When she handed me the change, I remembered the colonel in my car slouched over. His hand was between my thighs. The heat rose up between my breasts and flushed both cheeks. My heart was racing with my mind. I remembered the sunset . . . and him in the back of my car making love to me. I knew it wasn't a dream.

I dropped my head in shame.

"Hey! You okay? You're acting like you're the one taking this crew home."

I tried to breathe. I nodded. "I feel sick all of a sudden. Dizzy." It wasn't a lie. I could have fallen over or thrown up right there. "Can you handle these guys?" I faced Jenna with the few answers that gave me only more questions. "I need to get out of here."

"Yeah. Of course. Call me when you get home."

"I will. I'll call in a little bit." I kissed Liv and James and made them promise to be good.

"Love you, Mommy," Liv said and waved as I walked out the door.

I set the ice cream in my cup holder, and the wave of nausea returned. "What have we done?" I said to no one and drove to the colonel's house.

I parked next to his car and took my ice cream with me as I walked to the side door. I knocked. I kept breathing. The feel of his body against mine flooded me again, and I held on to the side of the house to steady myself.

He opened the door and pushed the screen out toward me. His police T-shirt stretched across his chest, and I wanted to touch him. I fought every need and focused on the one screaming for the truth. "Are you okay?" He pulled me inside.

I surveyed the empty house. "Are you alone?"

Vince walked in front of me. He was reading me the way I'd been watching him the last few months. He knew so much more than me. "Yes."

"Taste this." I shoved the ice cream toward him and fought back tears burning behind my eyes. Vince stared down at the cup in my hand. "Taste it," I said, and my voice cracked.

"Mar—"

"Mar." I started to cry at the name. How could I not have remembered it before? He used to call me Maris.

Vince moved faster than I could stop him. His arms were around me, but I moved back.

"How could I?" I faced him. I faced the unknown, and it

was crushing me with need and longing and disgust for what I'd never thought I was capable of. I took a spoonful of the ice cream from the cup and placed it in his mouth the same way he'd fed it to me as I drove us around in secrecy. I watched as he swallowed it, never taking his eyes off me. "You have to help me." The desperation in my words was too great for me to face.

"How?" he asked, and I wanted to cry.

"I need you to tell me the truth." The tears came. They ran down my face, and I closed my eyes. When I opened them, Vince was the one who looked like he was in pain. "I need you to tell me what I have become."

Vince shook his head, denying my judgements on the horrible wife I'd turned into sometime in the past year. No wonder I couldn't remember. I was too ashamed to face it.

"What have you remembered?" he asked, his voice tight like the strings of a guitar.

I leaned against the wall behind me, needing something solid to hold me up. "The way your thigh felt against mine on the school bus to Philadelphia." My eyes searched the room for my sanity. "How every day I inhale when you walk past me to trap as much of you inside my body as I can, because it warms me even when you're walking away." Vince stayed silent. His chest rose with every breath. "What your skin felt like beneath my hands." The ice cream was cold in my hand. "And tonight, I remembered making love to you in the back of my car."

I waited for the dam to break, for the tears and the screams of horror to come, but they left me staring at him and burning inside.

He took my face in his hands and searched my eyes for something, but he knew so much more about what was inside me than I did. He kissed me, and my head fell back to let him. His tongue in my mouth ignited something inside me. I wanted to climb up him. He forced me back against the wall and ground against me, and I knew to the center of my core what it felt like to make love to this man. He was a part of me.

I raised my hand to his chest and pressed against it.

He released me and took a step back. Self-hatred overcame my need for him. "You're not a whore."

I could barely face him. "Says the man I was having an affair with."

thirty

"WE CAN'T STAY HERE," VINCE said. He was watching the cars go by on the street in front of the house. "Someone will recognize your car."

"Stupid car."

"Do you remember the cabin?" His voice was soft and filled with patience.

"No." I only risked one word. My composure was fleeting. *Who am I?*

"I'll drive your car. I'll answer all your questions when we get there."

I let the question break through my silence. Tonight I would face my past, even if I couldn't face myself. "Why there?"

"Because that's where we used to meet. It can't be seen from the road."

The sick feeling of lying crept back into my throat. It sat there the same way it had when I'd found the cash in my tampon box. I followed him to my car. It was dark already, and I hoped no one recognized me with him. Vince moved the driver's seat back and drove out of his driveway. I waited to see which way he turned, hoping something would come back to me, but nothing did. He made a left after the lake and headed out of town.

"I talked to your wife last week."

He kept driving. I was sure he heard me, but only because I

was more sure of him than I was of myself.

"I swore to her that you weren't seeing anyone else. That no other woman calls you or comes to visit you at the station." The conversation replayed in my head and made me sick.

Vince reached across the truck seat and grabbed my hand. Love radiated from his touch and was followed by the realization it belonged to someone else. He was another woman's husband—not mine. I knew he was watching me, but I stared out the window into the darkness. I preferred it to the darkness in my mind.

My phone rang, and I searched through my bag to find it. "It's Jenna." I said before answering the call. "Hi," I said to her, remembering I was supposed to call her.

"Are you okay?"

"I am. It's just a headache."

"You should go back to your doctor. Have you had any others since the accident?"

"No. This is the first one, but I'll call him tomorrow."

"Promise me you're going to go to bed."

I glanced over at the colonel as he drove down the desolate road. "I promise. I'll call you in the morning. Good luck."

I hung up and stared down at my phone. The one I'd saved his number in under Jenna's name.

The colonel pulled onto a hidden lane and jumped out of the car to open a gate about fifteen feet off the road and in the woods. Once through it, he stopped again and locked it behind us. When he climbed back in the car, he looked at me expectantly, and I shook my head. Nothing. Not one memory came back of ever having been here.

I followed Vince into the cabin. I wrapped my arms across my chest to fight off the cold. Vince walked into the back room and came back out with a police sweatshirt for me to wear.

"I wasn't expecting you. I'll get the fire started."

I put the sweatshirt on and inhaled deeply Vince's scent

from its fabric.

"Would you like a beer or some whiskey?" he asked as he lit the corners of the newspaper he'd just stacked logs on top of.

A shot of heroin. Was anything strong enough to get me through this conversation? "I guess I'll start with a beer." I turned toward the refrigerator in the corner of the kitchen. "Can I get you one?" I didn't know if he drank, or if he drank beer. How could I know what his dick felt like in me, but not know if he liked beer? I was a whore.

"Yes. Thanks." He was still kneeling in front of the wood-burning stove, nursing the fire.

I used the bottle opener screwed to the wall and handed him one.

"Let's go in here," he said and led me into the adjacent room. It had a coffee table, a bunch of unmatched chairs, and three sets of bunk beds lining the walls.

"What is this place?"

He laughed. "That's the first thing you asked me the very first night you came here."

I turned to him, jealous of his memories. "When was that? When did *this* start?" I felt so safe with him. As if he could protect me from whatever I'd become.

"A little over a year ago was the first time." His eyes bore into me, threatening to swallow me with their intensity. "It was the first time we were here together."

"Where were we before that? How did this begin? What did I do?" The questions fell from my mouth. He had the answers to the questions I never thought I'd have to ask. He was the one with the information. The one I had sex with who wasn't my husband. He made me a whore, or I made him one. "Who else have you done this with? Why did I do this?" My voice was thick with the sobs that were forming in my chest. "What's wrong with me?"

"Come sit down."

I looked at the couch. I knew we'd had sex on it and probably every surface in this cabin, but I couldn't remember any of it. I walked around to the front of the couch and sat down. Vince sat on the coffee table facing me. His knees straddled mine, his face only inches from my own. I took a sip of my beer, seeking a little bit of control I'd completely lost, along with the rest of the last year. "Talk," I said.

He half-laughed at an inside joke I no longer understood. He was privy to our secret banter and the lost intimacy between us. I was jealous. "We met on the field trip." His leg touched mine the same way it had on the school bus. "I wanted to be near you. From the moment you walked into the classroom and stood all by yourself and ignored every other mother in there, I was attracted to you." I'd hoped not to speak to anyone, at least not about children, homework, carpool, and the dress code. "I'd never felt that way about another human being."

I lowered my head. A shallowness caved in my chest. I'd wanted him, too.

"I needed to spend more time with you," Vince continued. "But you said you weren't the type to have an affair." I sighed. I still wasn't the type. "I didn't care. I couldn't stop myself. I finagled a way into your pool club. I made sure I attended parties I knew you were going to, and I followed you to the shore. But you still wanted no parts of me."

I stayed still and memorized his words.

"And then there was an accident."

Goosebumps covered my arms. Fear. I felt fear, followed by the urge to pull him close to me.

"Do you remember the accident?"

I reached up and touched his face where the blood had run down it. He rested his head in my hand. "You scared me," I said with a weakened voice.

Vince closed his eyes. He was truly beautiful sitting with me. He was lovely and kind. But he wasn't mine.

I dropped my hand from his face, and he caught it by the wrist. He held it in his and traced his fingertips over my palm.

"Was I the reason you left your wife?"

He stopped caressing my hand. "No." I stared at him, not believing him, and he shook his head. "You were the reason I realized I needed to leave my wife, but even if we were never together, it was right. Lynn and I deserve better than what we had."

He closed his knees together, pressing our thighs against each other. I rested my hands on his legs. The heat traveled from my hands, up my arms, and down my body. He affected me.

"Did you love me?" Even without remembering, I knew I loved him. I knew it the first day I'd returned to work. I knew it at lunch with him, and I knew it in the car with his wife. I'd been in love with him as long as I'd known him. I didn't need my memory to know it.

Vince laughed.

"Is loving me funny?"

"Sometimes. Most of the time it's frustrating. I'm laughing because you made me promise never to fall in love with you." He rested his hands on top of mine on his thighs. "You tried everything to contain our relationship. To keep it manageable so you'd never be caught. You swore that the only way we could be together was if I never loved you."

"Did it work?" His answer terrified me. All I wanted was for him to love me, even if it was wrong.

Vince's hands moved up my arms, his heat settling beneath his fingers, warming me with every inch he touched. I watched as they caressed my shoulders, and I leaned my head back as they threaded in my hair. Vince leaned forward and touched his lips to my neck, setting me on fire. I inhaled deeply, trying to counteract the heat. His lips dragged up to my ear, and I brought my gaze down to meet his.

"No," he said and kissed me. His lips and tongue moved slowly, tasting me for the second time, and I didn't let myself think about anything but the way my body felt when he touched me. His tongue drove the warmth of Vincent Pratt back into me. He was everywhere. I could have lost myself in him, but he held me there in every way.

When he released me, I moved my hands to his chest. "Why didn't you tell me before now? Why not the day you came to see me in the hospital, or at the shore?"

"Because the last time we were together before you . . . fell" He paused and looked down as if he still wasn't convinced it was an accident. "Right before then, I promised you I'd never ask for another thing from you. I had told you that all you had to do was say the word and we'd be together, but that I'd never push you for more."

"But you knew how I felt about you? You knew how much you meant to me. Why not just tell me?"

The colonel covered my hands with his own before dropping them on my legs between us. "Because I knew loving me made you hate yourself."

I couldn't hide the confusion from my face. Loving him was one of my deepest memories, or feelings, that still remained inside me. It rested right between the shame of letting down my family and trading my children's happiness for my own. "I'm not the kind of woman who has an affair," I whispered.

"I know." He laughed a little, and the darkness lifted around us. "No one knows that better than me."

"I'm sorry I did this to you," I said, feeling responsible for the destruction of his family.

"I'm not."

"How could we . . ."

"I don't know. I need you to remember it, though. I need you to know how much we loved each other, how much we meant to each other." He held my face in his hands and kissed me. I didn't know if it was a memory, or a new emotion, but I loved him, and I knew I'd love him forever. "It's impossible living without you. I still won't ask you for a thing. If you're happy, then this is the way it'll stay. We'll work together and be friends, nothing more."

He held me in his stare, and I wanted to know everything else he was keeping from me. The colonel stood, and I felt like a little girl as he towered above me. I needed him to fix all of this. To make it right so we could be together without anyone being hurt, but that wasn't how life worked. It wasn't how affairs worked.

"I'd better take you home."

I had a thousand more questions to ask him, but I stayed silent. He was letting me go. Giving me a fresh start to release the guilt and love myself again, and for tonight, I was going to take it.

thirty-one

MY DRESS WAS PERFECT. MY shoes were perfect. Everything was perfect except my marriage. Brad seemed to buckle under his stress more and more each day, and the guilt of my part in the erosion of our marriage wore me down with him.

I kept my distance from the colonel. We slipped into a silent relationship that included none of the usual jovial exchanges. One day, Daniels mentioned the new coolness in the office, and I pretended to have no idea what he was talking about. Truthfully, the office felt too hot to me, getting hotter with every day I stayed silent. It was another reason I had to leave the job I loved as soon as my memory completely returned.

Little things had come back. I remembered how awesome Liv was, the Fall Festival the year before, and how Liv had won the costume contest. I had remembered standing in the middle of Main Street, talking to Jenna and the colonel's wife about an upcoming field trip. The one I wasn't going on because I was planning on spending the extra time in bed with the colonel. All of it made me blush. Most of it made me sick. But I loved him. I couldn't stop myself.

I checked the time on my computer again. I needed to leave a little early. I was having my hair and makeup professionally done for Brad's office holiday party. They held it in January to avoid the rush of the holidays. It also coincided with promotions, so for some, there was a lot to celebrate. Even the party seemed to cause him stress, which was funny, since I couldn't remember a time Brad wasn't ecstatic when an open bar was involved. For some reason he didn't want to attend this one. Amit's insistence was what finally convinced him to go.

I was hoping it would be good for us. In another lifetime, we loved celebrations and the dancing and drinking that went along with them. We just needed to find the Meredith and Brad who used to be the last couple on the dance floor. We needed to remember why we were together in the first place. I hoped the floor-length red dress with the slit up the side would help bring it all back.

THE FRIGID AIR FLEW IN the front door as I waved the sitter inside.

"Mrs. Walsh, you look beautiful!"

"Thank you, Alexis. It's Mr. Walsh's office party tonight."

"I love your dress."

"Me, too. Let's hope he loves it."

"Where is he? Mr. Walsh." Funny how a twenty-year-old girl easily made the connection that I was an island, but I was able to ignore it most of the time.

"The party's in Philadelphia, near his office. So I'm meeting him there."

"Oh. Well, drive careful."

"I will. See you in a few hours. We shouldn't be much later than midnight."

"Take your time. We'll be fine while you're gone." I bundled in my coat and grabbed my clutch off the counter in the kitchen. It was a forty-minute drive to the hotel, which was plenty of time to prioritize my goals for the evening.

I had to find some clue as to why my husband was so angry all the time and manage to find a way for us to have some fun together the way we used to. I wanted Brad to love me the same way he did before we moved out of the city. I wanted him to bring me home and *make* love to me, not just fuck me.

I wanted him to make me forget about the colonel. To make me forget who I was.

I felt like he'd succeeded in doing it at least once before, so he could do it again.

I pulled into the parking garage and found the closest spot to the elevator I could fit the enormous Escalade. Groups of people dressed in formal attire walked from their cars to the elevators. While Brad's boss' party was usually an intimate affair, this party was for the entire Philadelphia office and some counterparts from around the world. There would be several hundred people here. I shared the elevator with four couples. One I recognized from a party a few years ago.

"Meredith, right?"

"Yes." I shook the gentleman's hand. "I'm sorry. You look familiar, but I can't place your name."

"It's Richard, and this is my wife, Hillary."

"Of course. How have you been?" The elevator ride was long but good practice for what was coming my way.

"Good. How were the holidays?" A question I would undoubtedly repeat and answer fifty times over the next few hours. The elevator doors opened, and everyone exited together. We were all going to the same place.

"Busy. How about you and Brad? The kids must have been excited."

"Oh, they were." I followed Richard and Hillary to the coat check. The poor man had his own wife and now Brad's to deal with. As soon as possible, I made an excuse to go to the bathroom and relieve him of me.

I freshened up, smoothed my hair on the sides, and reapplied my lipstick. Brad was going to love the dress, and we were going to love each other. I checked my phone for texts about the kids and stored everything back in my clutch. Taking one last deep breath, I opened the door to find my husband.

It took about thirty seconds to see him after I entered the ballroom. He was at the bar, surrounded by people hanging on his every word. He was taller than almost every one of them. He glanced toward me and winked, and at that moment, I thought we were going to be okay.

I worked my way through the people until I was next to him. He was ordering me a glass of Cabernet, and when he tipped the bartender, I kissed him on the lips. Brad smiled before his eyes darted around the room, and my heart fell, cemented to a sinking brick of fear that daddy's friend, Dharma, was more than in Liv's head.

"I've been watching for you," he said and handed the wine glass to me.

"You have?" I wanted to love him. I wanted to need him the way I used to, or at least the way I thought I used to.

"Of course. You look beautiful."

They say that to everyone. I pushed my mother's words out of my head. "Thank you. Have you been here long?" Brad had that I'm-kind-of-drunk smile he often had after a few beers.

"A bunch of us went to happy hour before here."

"Hey, Meredith," Brad's friend, Amit, said just before pulling me into a hug. "How's that head of yours? We were worried."

"It's good." I laughed as I spoke. Amit and Brad had been close since Brad had started working there. He was at our wedding a million years ago.

"Did your memory come back?"

"Just about all of it," I said, and watched the smile drain from Brad's face. Fear replaced his unyielding confidence and it left me cold. "Everything I need to know is back."

We danced. We drank. We ate.

I listened to every word spoken around me for some hint as to the origin of Brad's stress. I still harbored some hope it was job related and not a result of another woman. Nothing came up. Amit seemed his laid-back, normal self. In fact, out of everyone who was at the party, Brad was the only one who seemed on edge.

He stayed close to me, barely leaving my side to get another drink. As the line formed by the coatroom, I excused myself to use the bathroom one last time before driving back to New Jersey. While I was in the restroom, I came up with the brilliant plan to convince Brad to leave his car at the hotel so we could drive home together. We could bring the kids into the city tomorrow to retrieve it. We'd be like a real married couple. Normal. Like he liked us.

However, when I came out of the bathroom, Brad was nowhere to be found.

I scanned the ballroom and he wasn't there. I checked both bars inside as well as the one set up in the hall. I knew he wasn't on the terrace smoking. Brad hated it. But after a few minutes of still not finding him, I walked over to the windows. Brad was leaning down toward the young girl who was speaking to him. She was petite with dark hair, which was pulled back in a sleek ponytail. Her head flipped back and forth violently as words flew from her mouth. At one point, she pointed a finger at him. She was maybe twenty-five, twenty-six. Quite junior to be so combative with Brad. Most people his level wouldn't dare speak to him that way.

I gently pressed the bar on the glass door and opened it.

"She's none of your fucking business," Brad said, and I stopped breathing. I stood in the doorway as both of them looked up at me. Neither of them spoke.

Instincts kicked in, and I smiled my fake, nice-to-meet-you smile I'd plastered on my face most of the night. "Sorry to interrupt."

"You're not," Brad said too fast. He stepped back from the girl.

"I'm Dharma," she said and walked over with her hand

outstretched, but I already knew who she was. Dharma had enormous breasts that were billowing from the top of her dress. Even as a heterosexual woman, my eyes were drawn to them.

"Meredith," I said, shaking her hand before turning to Brad. "Are you ready to go? It's getting late."

"You can't leave now. We were just going to the lobby bar for the after-party." Dharma wasn't talking to me, even though she was staring right at me. Her words were meant for Brad. She was bold and young.

"Would you excuse us?" Brad said to Dharma without using her name, as if by not saying it, I would forget she existed.

"Nice to meet you," she said and walked back inside.

"Would you mind if I stayed a little later?" Brad asked. He was sweating, but it was freezing out.

"I was actually hoping we could ride home together." Brad's shoulders rose as he tilted his head with denial. "Like a couple," I added and hated the way my voice sounded. If there was something to be jealous of Dharma for, I wasn't going to let Brad know it.

He leaned over the way he'd been with Dharma just minutes before and kissed my cheek. "I won't be late."

The cold wind whipped around us, taking the last shreds of affection I felt for my husband with it.

thirty-two

I DROVE OVER THE BRIDGE alone. It was almost funny. I was content. The pressure of loving Brad was gone. I was no longer searching for the answer to the question that had plagued me since I'd remembered having sex with the colonel. The question that kept me awake at night. How could I have an affair?

Watching Brad and his young friend tonight made me realize I wasn't cheating on a thing. He was no more my husband than I was his wife.

For a split second, I tried to convince myself I was overreacting and that Dharma was not fucking my husband, but deep down I knew.

My mind drifted to every sentence out of Brad's mouth since the accident. He wasn't frustrated by work. He was stressed out by his young girlfriend. That could only mean one thing—she wanted to be more than his girlfriend.

I followed the roads home without paying much attention to the other cars or the direction in which I traveled. At least I didn't until I reached the base of the bridge in New Jersey. Instead of driving to the house I couldn't wait to move out of, I ached to return to a place I'd made love to the colonel. I knew the way to the pasture. I knew it just like I knew exactly how his hand had felt between my thighs as I'd driven us there while he fed me ice cream. My children were home, though, and that was where I needed to be.

I PAID THE BABYSITTER. I checked on the kids. I kissed each one and tried to figure out what their future held. Something had fractured tonight in my resolve. I was no longer willing to stay married at all costs. I'd met Dharma, and now I knew the payment I would not make.

It was two thirty in the morning when I heard Brad enter our bedroom. He pushed the door open hard, and it banged against the wall. I shot up in bed, fearing for the children before I knew what was going on.

"What the hell! You're going to give me a heart attack."

"Fuck you," Brad said. His voice was low, void of any emotion besides hatred, and I braced myself for an argument.

"Whatever, Brad." I lay back down but didn't close my eyes. There would be no mercy tonight. I knew Brad wasn't just going to pass out.

"What is your fucking problem?" he asked, and a memory of him asking me those same words before shot into my head. We were at Jenna's, and I hated him. I chased the memory around in my mind until Brad interrupted by asking, "Seriously, what is your *fucking* problem?" He was standing over my side of the bed. He didn't frighten me. He repulsed me.

"I've got no problem. Go to bed, Brad."

"Oh, you've got no problem? Then why did you try to make me feel guilty tonight?"

I sat up in bed and turned on the light. I wanted to see his ridiculous face as we had this insane conversation. "I don't know what you're talking about. We had a great time tonight." My voice was filled with shock, which was for his benefit. In reality, I knew I didn't do anything to make him feel guilty. He did that all by himself.

"You're not as perfect as you think." He was more than

happy to make me aware of it.

"I never said I was perfect."

He stared at me. He didn't move. He just stood over me, pondering. "You're so beautiful," he said, and I thought he might cry. I closed my eyes and shook my head, trying to reconcile the fact that he could repulse me more.

"Just go to sleep. Please."

"I won't lose you, Meredith. I don't care what you're thinking or what you want. I'm not going to lose you."

Brad didn't realize I wasn't some twenty-five-year-old he was fucking. I was his wife, and I was already gone.

THE NEXT MORNING, I WOKE up before Brad and the kids. I went downstairs and made homemade French toast. I let the smell of the melting butter and cinnamon waft through the house until it dragged all of them from their pillows. The kids came running down, following their favorite scent, and sat at the island while I poured them glasses of milk to go with their breakfast.

Brad came down, looking like he'd just risen from a coffin. His eyes were bloodshot with shadows circling each one. It was impossible, but he actually appeared shorter. He'd lost some of himself last night. He sat in the seat vacated by the kids, who had scarfed down their breakfast and were now running out of the room chasing each other and screaming. Brad dropped his head into his hands and moaned.

"Rough one?" I asked. My voice was kind. It appeared I cared about him, which was exactly what I wanted him to think.

"I'm surprised you're still talking to me."

"Why wouldn't I be talking to you? I had a great time at your party."

He raised his head from his hands, and I kissed his cheek.

Brad just stared at me.

I placed a plate full of French toast in front of him and let the aroma rise up to him. "Milk?"

"I think I need some coffee."

I laughed a little to hide my utter hatred for him. "I'll make it. You get started on putting some food in you."

I made the coffee and sat with Brad while he drank it and ate breakfast. When he finished, he looked slightly renewed. "I do need to talk to you about something," I said, and Brad put his coffee cup down in front of him. He looked like he wanted to die this time.

"About last night?"

"Not specifically." I let the words linger. I let him fear what I knew and wallow in the anxiety of it. When even that began to bore me, I continued. "I'm worried about you drinking and driving so much."

Brad's shoulders fell as he exhaled. A smile crossed his face, and even though he was clearly wounded, there was a chance he was going to survive. "I'm okay."

"You're not. You're going to get a DUI, or worse, you're going to kill someone. If Jenna's accident taught us anything, it's that none of us are invincible."

"I'm not your drunk friend, Jenna."

"No. You're not. You're my drunk husband." He rolled his eyes. "Okay, maybe not a drunk, but you seem to think you're above any of the problems that come with drunk driving. We live too far away from everything for you to keep going like this."

"I'm fine."

"I think we should buy a house in the city."

"What?" He took another sip of his coffee and scowled at me.

"When we close on this house, we're going to have a large sum of money. I think we should use it as a down payment on a condo in the city."

He watched me, trying to decipher my motives.

"Then you'll be able to crash there when you've been drinking or working late, and we'll be able to take the kids in for nights during the summer or holidays. They'll love it. And I won't worry so much about you."

Brad stared at me for several minutes. I kept busy wiping down the counter in front of him and loading the dishes in the dishwasher. The idea made perfect sense to me. I wouldn't want anything to happen to him.

"If not, you need to increase your life insurance."

Brad and I both laughed. I wasn't kidding, though.

thirty-three

JANUARY SETTLED INTO THE QUIET month it always was. Things returned to our normal. Our new house was coming along. The renovations were scheduled to be done by March, and we'd had several showings of our current house. Brad was depressed, and it seemed as if the enormous and cold house was a symbol of something greater to him, but he never talked about it.

I would just be happy to be out of it. I packed up the Christmas decorations and drove them to the basement of our new house. I stored them under the staircase, where the previous owner's Christmas tree had been. I remembered the purse I'd bought for myself for Christmas the year before and wondered if I knew even then. If, before my accident, I knew he was having an affair. Maybe that was why I'd allowed myself to have one.

Even if that were the case, it didn't excuse me. Brad having an affair was typical. My affair was disturbing. I'd never been the type. I'd never even considered it a possibility. How had my life gone so off course in such a short time?

Brad's attention seemed to be forever on his phone. He silenced it, there was never an interruption of a ding or some other annoying notification of infidelity, but it was always a part of our time together. Brad checked it often and whatever he read always seemed to anger him. He was out of his element.

Things usually worked out for Brad. It was like watching an out-of-practice musician trying to play. Brad had no idea who he was dealing with in Dharma.

When a married man had an affair with a young girl, he was the only one having an affair. She was dating.

Dharma was going to be a problem—for all of us.

I ignored Brad and his phone. I kept the smile glued to my face, determined not to let Brad know anything had changed about my commitment to our marriage.

I EXITED MY WARM CAR and practically ran to the police station. The wind chill was negative eleven, and the pain on my cheeks as the wind whipped against them confirmed the forecast. I set my bag down on top of my desk and left my coat on as I entered the break room and placed a mug full of water into the microwave for hot tea.

"Morning," the colonel said as he walked into the room. "Are you warm enough in here? I can turn up the heat."

I turned to him and raised my eyebrows. I knew he could make it hotter. He only smiled and poured himself a cup of coffee. We were alone in the station, and always alone in my mind.

"Do you feel safe with me?" I asked.

He was in the middle of sipping the steaming coffee. He moved it from his lips and watched me for some explanation.

I shrugged, trying to legitimize the question. "Like, when you're with me, do you have a sense of safety?"

A small laugh slipped from his lips, and it mesmerized me. "I know what you're asking. I'm just trying to figure out why you're asking. Do you not feel safe?"

I looked down. I wasn't sure why I was asking. It was just every time he was within five feet of me, I felt warm, secure, and calm. I couldn't imagine I had anywhere near the same effect on him, and I felt bad for him because of it. As if I owed him something, because he made me feel good. Everyone should feel the way I did when he was near me.

"I was just wondering." I avoided his question. I knew how much he enjoyed evasiveness.

"I don't *not* feel safe with you. But that's not the prevailing sense I have when you're near me."

We faced each other in the break room. Silence fell between us, and I let the need for him overtake me. It conjured up the memory of standing in my kitchen and crying as he left me.

"What is it?" he asked.

"Hug me."

He glanced at the hallway and up at the clock. His movements were slow as he placed his coffee on the counter, and I reached across to put my tea next to it. Vince moved within inches of me and wrapped his arms around my shoulders. He pulled me tight against him, and I inhaled him. I turned my head and let my face rest near his neck. His heartbeat was slow and pulsed heat through me. My arms tightened behind his back.

I stayed quiet and fell into my thoughts and my overwhelming need for him. We were standing on a dock together. It was warm out, and we were dancing. I closed my eyes, yearning to be back there. Then fear slipped between us, and I stiffened in Vince's arms.

"What?" His lips grazed the top of my head. I could have lain down with him. Forever.

"I remember dancing with you." Vince ran his hands through my hair, and the fear solidified in my mind. "I was terrified to lose you."

My cell phone rang at my desk. The sound of it barely penetrated the rare moment of peace and privacy with Vince, but the phone was my only connection to Liv and James when they weren't with me. I could hear it a mile away.

I released Vince from my arms and ran to my bag. The

school nurse's number flashed on my screen. This was never a good call.

"Hello," I said, not hiding the doom in my voice.

"Mrs. Walsh?"

"Yes. This is Mrs. Walsh."

"This is Marcia Carter, the nurse at the elementary school. Olivia's here in my office. She just threw up. Can you come get her?"

"Oh, no. Of course. I'll be right there." Poor Liv.

Poor me.

I put my coat on and locked my computer. When I walked back to the break room, he was smiling, having heard my conversation and recognized the gist of it.

"I have to go."

"I know."

"I'm sorry."

"No need to be. Your children need you. You've always made it clear, they come first."

I wasn't sure if he was talking about just the job, but I didn't ask. I just turned and walked out the door.

By the time I drove the mile and a half to the school, Liv had already thrown up again. I carried her feverish little body to my car and buckled her in the back. "I love you," I said and kissed her forehead.

"I love you, too, Mommy."

I closed her door and rushed to the driver's side. When I climbed in, she smiled at me as if she felt a little better. "Rough day, huh?" I said, watching her in the rearview mirror as I pulled out of the school's lot.

"I'm just glad I threw up in the nurse's office. Nick Louden threw up in class last month and everyone saw it. It had green lumps in it."

"Okay. I get the picture."

"I'm just saying. I'm glad that didn't happen to me."

"Me too."

Liv and I rode in silence through the center of town and back to our house. When I turned into our development, she said, "You know what else happened today?"

"What?"

"Evan tried to tell me I wasn't as awesome as I think I am."

I stopped the car halfway down our driveway. This had been my greatest fear since she'd begun the "I'm awesome" campaign of self-promotion. That someone, particularly a boy, would knock her off her peg.

"I think he was kidding," she said and nodded as she stared out the window.

I exhaled and drove the Escalade forward. "You sure you're okay?"

"Yeah. He had to have been kidding." Liv's eyes remained on the woods surrounding our house. "I'm awesome," she said to no one in particular, and I pulled the car into our garage.

thirty-four

JAMES WAS SAYING SOMETHING AS we drove to Jenna's house. It was barely audible from the third row of the Escalade, and even without hearing him, I knew it was probably a question.

I turned down the music and asked him to repeat it. "Nice and loud, so I can hear you all the way up here."

"What's a credit score?"

I took a deep breath and exhaled. "It's a number that represents how good a job you've done of borrowing and paying back money. It tells companies that may lend you money in the future if you're a good risk, meaning that you pay your bills on time or a bad risk, meaning that you don't pay them on time." James stared out the window as I spoke, deeply concentrating on what I was saying. I thought. "The score follows you everywhere and is used when you put in an application to rent an apartment. It's also considered for your car and health insurance rates, because it's one factor that demonstrates your character."

"Can someone steal your credit score?"

"No, but someone can steal your identity and ruin your credit score." I stopped talking. My head began to hurt, and I really hoped he didn't have any more follow-up questions. "Does that make sense?" I asked, praying the answer would be yes.

"It's so clear I can see through it."

"Okay," I said and turned up the radio.

I escaped the other questions swirling in their heads the rest of the drive. I parked in Jenna's driveway and the kids both flew out of my car. John was outside, loading up the back of his truck.

"Are you sure you're up to this?" I asked him.

"No," he said and laughed. I opened the lift gate on the Escalade and removed the sleds Santa had brought each of my kids. "We'll be fine. My brother and nephew are coming. He's sixteen."

"My kids are excited. And when they're excited, they talk a lot."

"I know." John laughed again. "I'm just worried I won't know the answers to all their questions."

"Oh, I never do. I make them search Google for things I can't answer. God, please let Google be right."

Jenna rushed out the door, kissed John, grabbed my arm, and said, "Let's go. Before they see me leaving." She climbed up into the passenger side of the Escalade and left John and I standing in her driveway.

"She needs to get away for a few hours," he said.

"Or days," I added. "I bundled them up. They'll complain the minute they're cold." Brad would say that was all my fault because I "kept them in a bubble." "Call me if you need anything."

I got in the car and drove back down Jenna's driveway before she said a word. By the time we were pulling onto the main road, she was relaxed. She cracked her window and lit a cigarette, and I didn't mind.

"So what do you need to do at the mall?" I asked. Jenna had called and told me we needed to go to the mall and lunch. All of which sounded like a dream. But when she said John would take the kids sledding, I feared I was imagining the whole phone call.

Jenna took an emerald ring from her wallet. It was a round stone surrounded by diamonds with diamonds down the sides as well. "I need to have this sized." She handed the ring to me.

"Wow! When did you get it?"

"For Christmas, but it's too big. I've never worn it."

"Tragic," I said and handed her back the ring, which she put on her finger and admired.

"And because I had to get out of my house. Do you have any idea how hard it is to raise three boys *and* be sober?"

"No," I said and laughed. "But if anyone can survive it, it's you."

We parked on the far side of the mall. The immense lot allowed the frigid air to whip around us as we rushed to the entrance. It was a cold day, even for sledding.

"Do you think they'll be okay?"

"Yeah. John will send them down the hill a few times, and once they start to freeze, he'll take them out for pancakes at the diner."

"Oh, good. I was hoping it wasn't going to be a long day."

"No. John gets it."

I followed Jenna to the jewelry store and perused the glass cabinets full of jewelry as Jenna talked to the sales associate about resizing her ring.

A man who reminded me of my high school principal faced me from behind the counter. "Can I help you with something?"

"No. I'm just looking. I'm here with my friend." I pointed at Jenna.

"Are you sure? Valentine's Day is coming. You can pick something out, and I'll make sure your valentine knows about it." The nametag on his chest said Chris Remster.

I shook my head. "No. Thank you."

"Your ring is breathtaking," he said to me as Jenna walked up beside me.

The only ring on my hands was my engagement ring. It was

pretty, but the man's reaction seemed a bit over the top. His pitch continued as he held my hand in his and tilted my ring toward the lights above us.

"Thanks," I said and took my hand back.

"May I clean it for you?" Mr. Remster asked, and I was confused.

"Let him clean it," Jenna said, and after I handed it over to him and he walked away, she added, "It's free."

"It's weird. Did you get your ring sized?"

"Yes. We get to come back in five to seven days."

"Perfect. Where do you want to eat?"

He came back with my ring and another salesperson. "It's quite unusual to see a blue diamond of this caliber and size," Mr. Remster said.

I shook my head and prepared to correct him when the other salesperson added, "It's exquisite."

"What? It's a blue topaz," I said. Brad knew me well enough to know a diamond was not for me.

They both laughed. "It's without a doubt a blue diamond. It's also incredibly valuable. It should be insured."

"This is not a topaz?" I asked again, looking down at the ring I'd worn since Brad had proposed.

"Did you inherit it?" Because of course, it must have been bequeathed to me. What other explanation could there have been for me not knowing that I was walking around with a blue diamond on my hand?

"Sort of," was all I said. I needed to get out of there. With a small smile, I grabbed Jenna by the elbow and guided her out of the store.

We walked to the Cheesecake Factory, and she didn't mention my ring until we were seated at the table and had ordered our meals. Then she hit me with it.

"How could you not know your ring is a blue diamond? I didn't even know there was such a thing." Her eyes bore into me. "Let me see it."

I took the ring off and dropped it in Jenna's hand. "I told Brad how I felt about diamonds. That so many people were being killed for the mining and sale of them that I refused to encourage more violence by feeding the industry with our money." Jenna looked at me as if she'd never heard the term "blood diamond" before. "It doesn't matter why I didn't want a diamond, what matters is that Brad knew it, but for some crazy ass reason he bought one anyway and lied to me about it."

"Okay," she said. Still not as appalled as me. The ring had won her over.

It hit me then that it wasn't that Brad never listened to me. No, he heard every word I'd ever said. He just didn't care.

"I'm thinking about getting a tattoo," I said.

Jenna handed me back the ring and looked down at her menu without another word, and I didn't explain. Brad was going to hear me, and he wasn't going to like what I had to say.

thirty-five

LYNN PRATT ENTERED THE POLICE station like a spring flower blooming. It was unseasonably warm that day, reaching almost to the high fifties and melting a large portion of the snow that surrounded us. Lynn wore skinny jeans, a turtleneck, and a slim gray blazer. She had a multi-chain necklace on that swung as she walked and drew attention to the current trend she was embracing. Her hair was highlighted and blown straight. I almost didn't recognize her.

"Hello," I said and worked hard to wipe the shock from my face.

"Morning. How are you?" she asked, and I continued to appraise her.

"I'm good." Her purse was new. It was a cross-body bag I'd seen in the mall the day I went in search of my dress for Brad's party. It was expensive and gorgeous. Perhaps it was a Christmas gift. "Lynn, you look great." I tried not to sound amazed. As if this version of Lynn couldn't be reconciled with the frazzled, unkempt one I'd known before.

"Thanks. It's taken a while, but I'm finally pulling myself back together." At the mention of her relationship with the colonel, I shut down. I couldn't hold up any part of that conversation. "It's like I've found a part of myself I hadn't known was missing."

The chief came out of his office and leaned on the

doorjamb. Lynn and I both looked at him. How must it feel to face us both? His wife and his lover, neither of which he was currently with, but both of whom he loved.

"I'm going to run out and get some lunch. Can I get you guys anything?"

They just stared at each other, and I couldn't get my purse fast enough.

"No, thanks," the colonel finally said.

"Okay," I said to no one, because no one was listening to me. I'd been completely lodged in their marriage the year before, and I wouldn't let myself be anywhere near the middle of it today.

I couldn't manage a thought until I was safely in my car. I looked at the clock on the dash. It was nine thirty in the morning, hardly lunchtime, not that anyone in the station cared. I drove home and sat in my car in my driveway. I read the news on my phone. Like, *all* the news. Every single story on CNN. I checked the weather for the next few days, and the extended forecast. When I ran out of stuff to read there, I went onto Facebook and floated around there until my phone rang.

It was a call from the colonel's desk phone.

"Hello?" I asked, because apparently I no longer knew how to answer a phone.

"Meredith?" He sounded drained.

"Yes."

"You can come back now."

I exhaled. He knew I was somewhere avoiding being there. "Thanks. I'll be right there."

"Take your time."

"Would you like to go to lunch with me?" I pulled the phone away from my ear and looked at it as if it had asked the question, not me.

What am I doing?

"Just friends," I said as I placed it back to my ear.

"I would love that. Just friends." His voice was quiet.

***

WE WENT TO THE DINER right in the middle of town. We sat in a booth by the window and watched as half the town walked on the sidewalk in front of us. The server and everyone sitting at the bar knew the colonel. They all said hello, and he introduced me to each one as, "Meredith Walsh, a former U.S. Attorney who now works with me at the police station." It was intoxicating.

"We never went out in public, did we?" My voice was low, but I wasn't whispering. We had no secrets. We were no longer breaking any laws.

"No. Never."

"I like this better," I said and continued to read my menu.

"That's because you don't remember."

I looked over my menu, and the colonel was challenging me with a naughty expression on his face. "Why, colonel." He was even more irresistible when he was playful. I wanted him to touch me. In the Riversbend Diner, I wanted him to put his hands on me everywhere. I took a deep breath. I believed him when he said I preferred it.

"I'm just telling you the truth. We always promised to be honest with each other."

I stared out the window again, searching for the memory of that or any other promise we may have made to each other. The only thing that came was a vague memory of James's camping trip. A sick feeling somehow attached to pitching a tent and replacing the batteries in his flashlight for tag.

"Lynn looked good." I changed the subject. Back to a safer one. I thought.

"She's moving on. She wants a divorce."

I dropped my menu to the table and stared at the colonel in disbelief. He lowered his menu and met my eyes with his own.

If only I could have hugged him. "Are you okay?"

The colonel nodded. "It's a relief. I'm glad she's happy."

"She met someone else?"

"How did you know?"

"Because I think that's what would make her happy."

"She's been talking to a guy we graduated Penn State with."

"How do you feel about that?"

"I'm not sure yet. It's all very bizarre. But I like him."

"You're such a good man." The comment was absurd. I was talking to my ex-lover about his estranged wife and her new boyfriend. That didn't make it any less true though. He was too good, better than anyone I'd ever known. He forced me to love him just by being himself.

thirty-six

I SEARCHED THROUGH MY WALLET for cash. I needed four dollars to attach to the permission slip for James's class trip. I found three dollars and seventy-five cents. "I know I have more money in here somewhere."

James hopped up on the stool next to the counter. "Do you want me to look?"

"Yes." I rummaged through the notebook and folders for the spring fair in my purse hoping a dollar had fallen between them, and James searched through all the compartments of my oversized wallet. He wasn't going to find anything. I hated Mondays.

"What's this?" James held up a penny with the center missing. I stood up straight—the memory holding me above the ground.

"It's a lucky penny," I said and took it from James. I held it in my hand. The center was cut out in the shape of a heart.

"Cool!" James said and took the penny back. "Can I have it?"

My past exploded in my mind. The first night I was with the colonel at his hunting cabin. The book club I lied about in Philadelphia. His truck, my Escalade, this penny . . .

"Here," I said and handed the penny to James. "We've got to go." I barely heard the words as they left my mouth. "Liv, get in the car. We're going to be late for school."

James followed me out yelling, "Mom, wait!" I stopped.

Mentally, I was barely there. "Take this with you. I want you to have the luck." He placed the penny in my palm and climbed into the back of my car.

I sat in the driver's seat and squeezed the penny in my hand. The day Vince had first told me he loved me and gave me this penny shot through me. I'd been angry at the time and hurtful when I'd left him. I was terrified of losing him.

I closed my eyes. I loved him now. I knew I'd loved him then. It wasn't just an affair. The outrage at the kids' principle over the dress code. Vince fucking me on the hood of his police cruiser. Dancing with him on the dock at Lake George all came back. It was always him. It was never an affair. It was Vincent Pratt.

Liv hauled her backpack, flute, and lunchbox into the backseat and pulled her door shut. We drove to their school without another word. As if my children could sense I needed silence to breathe.

"Have a great day," I managed to say as they hopped out of the car. "I love you." The words lingered behind them. They walked through the front door of their school and I sat motionless in the carpool line. Lost in my thoughts in the Escalade their father had purchased for me.

"Let's move it," Mr. Danner yelled in my window, making me jump and press on the accelerator. I left my children and drove to the police station.

The frozen air surrounding me barely penetrated my sweater dress and boots. My coat I left in the car. All I needed was Vince. I steadied my breathing and tried to calm down as I opened the door to the station. The vision of him naked and lying next to me in a hotel room in Philadelphia hit me and my thighs tightened together. I took a deep breath.

"Hey, Meredith. What brings you in on your day off?" Thompson asked.

"Is the chief here? I need to talk to him." It was as if

someone else was speaking the words.

"Took the day off. I think he's hunting. Do you want me to call him?"

Yes, call him and get him here right now! I wanted to scream. "No. It can wait. I was just driving by. I'll talk to him the next time I'm in."

"Okay."

"Be safe," I said and walked back out the door I'd just come in.

I sat in my car with my phone in my hand. I could call him. My finger slid across the screen. My memories guided me to the icon for "Private Mode." I followed the directions and swiped my finger over the home button, allowing the phone to read my fingerprint.

Tears filled my eyes as I opened the private photo album. The first picture was the colonel at his cabin. He had no shirt on and the sweetest smile on his face. It was the same smile he'd had when I'd answered the door at my shore house after I'd hurt my head.

Liv swinging in my backyard skipped through my mind. She'd been going so high. I'd made Brad come watch her, and then he'd said, "Say the word," and the world stopped around me. I'd thought he knew about Vince and me. I'd been terrified he'd take Liv and James away forever.

I put the car in drive and paused as I remembered Brad screaming at me not to walk away from him. He'd been completely out of control.

"Shh. The kids will hear you," I'd said, trying to calm him down.

"I will not quiet the *fuck* down!" he'd screamed at me, and I'd turned and walked out of the room with him an inch behind my every step. I stayed calm. I still didn't know what he knew, but he wasn't learning anything else from me. I climbed the front staircase, a few steps ahead of him. "You're not going anywhere!" he'd yelled and yanked my ankle out from under me.

Brad would never let me go. He would never lose . . . me.

thirty-seven

I DROVE TO THE HUNTING cabin. The one I'd been to at least once a month for a year. The one I'd first made love to him at. I hated him for not telling me sooner. He should have told me the day he came to the hospital or the day we were together at the shore. He should have done something to make me remember.

> You can't be held captive
> If you can't be caught.

The words on his card rang in my head and reminded me of how he understood me better than anyone else alive. I loved him more than I hated him. He'd promised me he would never ask for another thing, and he kept that promise until I'd almost lost him in my mind forever.

I wanted to scream at him and punch him for leaving me alone. I inhaled deeply, my breath catching as I exhaled and tried to grasp the coronel in my mind. I wanted to fuck him until I couldn't remember the other man in my life, and then I wanted to fall asleep in his arms.

I wanted him.

The road was as familiar as my driveway. The clarity was overwhelming. Tears filled my eyes as the memory of the night we'd spent together on a lake in New York filled my mind.

Anger had seared through me at the thought of him leaving his wife. And now that he'd done just that, guilt overcame me.

From the road, I could see the gate to the cabin lane was wide open. I pulled off and stopped just inside the opening, put the Escalade in park, and took a deep breath. Too much had happened. More than one person could forgive or forget, and he was willing to let me live without the memory of him for the rest of my life if that meant I was happy.

I stepped out of the vehicle and swung the gate shut. I closed the padlock and locked us away from the world. This had been our haven for almost a year, and now I returned, needing to feel safe again.

The colonel's truck was covered in frost and parked near the walk leading up to the cabin. I stood still and listened for movement in the woods. Squirrels scurried around and up a tree. They chased each other across a branch and leaped onto the tree next to me. But other than their pursuit, the world was silent.

My gaze fell on the door, and my anger at his silence returned. I was going to walk in there and scream at him. I was going to throw back in his face his insistence that we *never* stop talking and that we work through things together. That was what he'd made me promise. That we would never shut each other out again, but he deserted me. He broke that promise and left me alone to find my own way through this sea of deceit.

I marched toward it. The doorknob in my grasp sent a wave of need through my body. The familiarity of it in my hand, the entry into a place it was safe to touch him. To have him to myself. The feelings calmed me, but even the peace left me off balance.

It was too much to process. Love, hate, betrayal. Vince. Brad. All the things I never understood suddenly all made sense, and none of them were a part of my plan for myself.

I turned the knob and stepped inside to the four walls that

protected the clandestine truth of my life. Silence filled the room. It surrounded me and held me tight against the door I'd just closed behind me. My hand lingered on the knob, waiting for him to tell me what to do. Vince would know what to say. He'd halt the chaos in my mind and replace it with the warmth that always surrounded him.

Cool air caressed my neck, and I shivered, still waiting for him. The wood stove had burned its logs from the night before and now sat quiet in the corner of the room, the log bin loaded next to it. He'd told me a dozen times, "It'll warm up in a minute. Let me get the fire going."

He must be out hunting.

I'd sit on the couch where he'd made love to me until he returned. But I stopped as soon as I stepped into the second room of the cabin. Vince was lying on the couch with the television on low. His left arm was on top of the blanket, exposing half his chest and arresting my breathing. His eyes were closed, and he hadn't shaved in a few days. I leaned against the doorframe and watched his chest rise and fall as he lay motionless and alone.

"You are the finest man I have ever known, and I will love you forever," I whispered, and he still didn't move.

I stepped out of my boots, watching for him to wake up, and left them by the wall. My clothes I dropped in a pile on the chair, and I crawled under the blanket next to Vince. The couch was small and he took up most of it, but he was warm and solid, exactly how I remembered him. I inhaled deeply and closed my eyes.

Vince stirred, raising his arm over me and pulling me closer to him. He rolled slightly onto his side and kissed the top of my head, as if I'd slept with him a thousand times before rather than only one night.

He thinks I'm Lynn.

Bitter disgust sunk down into me until he said, "Maris," and the feeling was replaced by something so far beyond love

I couldn't fathom a term to define it. It was a mix of devotion, desire, adoration, and a complete trust that I'd never experienced in my life before I met this man.

"Vince." My voice was quiet. I didn't want to startle him, but I wanted him to wake up. I kissed his chest and ran my fingertips down his arm. "Vince, wake up."

His breathing halted. The muscles of his upper body tightened beneath me, and I stayed still. "Vince. It's me." His eyes opened, and I waited for his recognition, but he only stared at the wood beams above us. "It's Meredith." My resolve cracked under the weight of my name. The desperation I felt withered my words to the point I barely recognized my own voice, and his breath lifted his chest beneath my hand. "Vince—"

"Shh." He tightened his arm around my shoulders. His heartbeat pounded beneath my ear. I inhaled deeply and let myself disappear into the safety of Vincent Pratt. The anger at him for not telling me was gone. The need to scream at him was lost forever. I just wanted to be near him.

He lifted me on top of him, and I raised my head to face the most patient man I'd ever known. His stare fell from my eyes to my lips as his hands dragged down my body and back up again.

"Vince," I started, but the look in his eyes stole the words from my mind. I stayed quiet in his arms, waiting for him to believe I was there. He didn't move, and neither did I. His silence was breaking my heart.

"I remember," I said, and through his eyes, I could see clear to his soul. And I felt, without a sliver of doubt, that he loved me in a way I'd forgotten was possible. He was more than I deserved.

"I know this is a dream, and I don't care." His voice was rough, barely of this world, but then again, neither were we. The desperation of our union was locked away with us in this cabin in the woods. We would never exist in the light, and because of one fight with Brad, we'd almost disappeared from the darkness.

My breasts rested on his chest, and I lowered my head to see our naked bodies touching for the first time in months. A heat originated in each nipple and spread through my core, throbbing between my legs, and I let them each fall to his sides as I tightened them against his waist. Vince held me tight to him as he sat up and the blankets fell away. My legs tangled behind his and my arms rested around his neck. Every muscle in my body tightened as I finally felt him.

Vince's lips dragged along my chin. His hot breath followed his mouth to my ear. His tongue toyed with my ear lobe, and I dropped my head back, letting the sensation of his lips on my skin spread through my body until my hips pressed against him. "Do you remember this?" he asked. I forced my eyes open as I watched him take my nipple between his teeth. I was on fire. It was strumming under my skin, replacing the calm he always brought me with a frenzied need pounding between my legs, against my chest, and in the back of my throat.

"Talk to me."

I threaded my fingers through his hair. "I remember."

His fingertips slid down my stomach and between my legs. He slipped two into me and paused. His breath found my ear, and I trembled from his touch. "Do you remember this?" My eyes closed as he pushed his fingers deeper inside of me and they collided with the demand for him to touch me there. "Meredith?"

I fought to inhale. "I remember." In his arms, I was in heaven. I pulled him closer with my legs around his back and my arms locked around his neck. I wanted him. On top of me, inside of me, lying next to me. Until death do us part.

"I've waited so long," he said, but I could barely hear him. His fingers pressing inside of me stole all my senses and focused them on the heat pulsing at the point of his touch.

I reached down. It was as if his dick had never left my hand.

I stroked it. I knew how to touch him. He was mine, and when he moaned, I rose up on my knees and guided him into me. "I'm here." Not a moment had passed since the last time I'd made love to him. Not a minute had been missed.

Vince lifted me up and pressed me down again. Thrusting his dick even farther inside of me, and I stopped there. I faced him, faced *this*. Nothing would ever change the way I needed him.

Vince pressed his lips hard against mine. He kissed me until I was back in this cabin for the first time. When guilt had abandoned me to my beautiful colonel.

"I love you," he said and held me as he pushed me on my back and climbed on top of me. "I love you."

He spread my legs wide and crashed into me again, igniting waves of need that spread through me. He held me tight, thrusting against me, marking me forever, and robbing me of a future without him. I dug my fingers into him trying to hold off the release I'd sought every day I was near him. With every movement of his body to mine, I gave myself to him a little more until there was nothing left but him.

When the heat began to choke me and the trembles turned to tremors, I said, "I'm going to come," but Vince didn't respond. He was lost inside of me. His body finally taking what we'd both needed for months. He was rough and powerful, but I'd never felt as safe as I did in his arms. I belonged right here with him.

Vince made love to me until neither of us could speak. My orgasms had run away with my ability to think. They'd stolen any recognition of anything other than that of his body touching mine.

He lay beside me, cradling me in his arms, and the torrent of emotions the vision of him sleeping had held back, crashed against me. There was no place left to hide. In the silence of the cabin, safely wrapped in his arms, I cried for the lost memory of us.

thirty-eight

THE COOL AIR FLICKED AGAINST my now-electrified skin until I shivered. Vince pulled me on top of him, covering us with the blankets and nuzzling me closer to him than humanly possible. He caressed my face with his thumbs, erasing the stray tears. He was everywhere—below me, next to me, in my heart, and in my mind. I took a deep breath, still grateful for my memory.

I lay on top of him listening to his heart beating against my cheek. I breathed in the rich mahogany scent and disappeared into the safety of Vincent Pratt. It would be a while, if ever, that I was with him again.

"Vince—"

"Don't say it." His arms tightened around me, and I inhaled, wanting to trap him inside me.

"I can't go back. I can barely face your wife now." I lifted my head from his chest, already knowing I was never going to be able to walk out of here.

"I can't go on with you living in that house." His voice was dark, filled with a hatred I'd never seen before in him. He pulled me up to face him and demanded, "Look me in the eyes when you answer this question." I already knew what it was about. "Did he hurt you?"

"No." I stared steadily at him. I already had a plan for Brad, and it didn't include the colonel.

"You promised you'd always be one hundred percent honest."

"I was watching Liv swing. He came up behind me and said we could move if I wanted to." Vince waited, observing every breath from my lungs to my lips. "Brad put his hands around my neck and said, 'Just say the word.'"

I steadied my breathing. I didn't let Vince see the tears swirling just below my surface. The memory of that moment, the end of Vince and the weeks after it when I barely knew him, came back and hurt me all over again.

"How did he know?"

"I don't know. I think from the text I sent you the day of the talent show. I didn't erase it immediately. There was a lot going on that day."

"What happened after he said it?"

"Am I being interrogated?"

"Yes. I almost killed him just for being in the house when you were injured."

"He walked away. I sent the e-mail to you and checked for anything else on my phone that needed to be deleted."

"And?" Vince wasn't letting it go.

"And he started screaming at me. I told him to be quiet so the kids wouldn't hear. I acted like he was crazy, which was easy because of the way he was screaming."

Vince's muscles tensed beneath me. "And?"

"And I walked up the stairs with him following me. I fell. My feet came out from under me. I was rushing." Vince stared at me, demanding the truth, but the words I'd shared were not a lie. "He didn't hit me with a baseball bat. Why did you think he did?"

"Your e-mail. Your injury. And when I went to your house, the contents of your purse were all over the kitchen counter as if he'd searched your bag."

I looked around the cabin. Brad was going to be harder to

take care of than I'd thought. I couldn't underestimate him.

With two fingers on my chin, Vince tilted my head to face him again. "If I find out you're covering for him . . ."

"You'll what? Hit me with a baseball bat?"

"Not you. And I won't need a bat."

I kissed Vince. I knew I had to leave. I had to go back to my house. It must have felt like a good-bye to him, because he rolled me over, trapping me beneath him again.

"What happens now?" he asked.

"I need some time. I have to take care of some things."

"What things?"

"My family."

Vince ran his fingers through my hair, and I could feel his frustration in the taut muscles of his arms. Guilt lowered my eyes from him. He still wasn't mine to have. Nothing had changed about our situation, and although I wanted him, I wouldn't put us through the last year all over again. Too much had already been lost to go back.

"Do me a favor?"

"Anything," he said and lifted my head to face him.

"Stay off Facebook for a while."

"What are you going to do?"

I couldn't include him in this. It was between my husband and me. "I have to go. I'm sorry."

"I know." Vince rolled off me, letting me sit up and catch my breath. I wasn't sure I could stand. The totality of the morning left me weak. I could have lain back down with him and fallen asleep safe in his arms, but that was impossible. I dressed while he watched me in silence. He was sitting on the couch, and I knew I'd never survive without him.

When he stood, I turned to face him.

"Vince." He looked at me, intrigued by my use of his name. "I love you." I broke through his wall of regret, and he smiled and shook his head slightly. "I love you, and now, we know that's never going to change." He stayed still, watching me. "I'd lost you in my mind, but every day I knew that I loved you even when I didn't know myself."

He leaned down and grazed my ear with his lips. His breath on my skin melted me.

"I love you," I repeated. "But I still can't have an affair with you. If our future's together, it shouldn't include anyone else. Because that's not real life."

thirty-nine

I'D ALWAYS BEEN OPEN WITH my phone and had always left it out. The kids knew the passcode pattern. Anyone could use it, because I wasn't using it for anything other than a tool to mother my children.

Brad, in contrast, never left his phone unattended. I checked it while he was in the shower and tried a password every other day. I never guessed correctly. When it vibrated on our nightstand, I checked to see who was contacting him, but he had it set so nothing showed on the screen.

I didn't actually need the information. I was pretty clear on Dharma's role in our lives. I was just hoping one of them was dumb enough to make this easier for me. I spent my day off in our home office, scouring our phone records for repeated numbers. I'd never checked it for anything before. It took about three seconds to identify Dharma's number.

A quick visit to Google, and I had her LinkedIn profile and the address of her apartment in center city. She was as young as she looked. Give or take a few extra years to finish college, Dharma was twenty-six years old.

I leaned back in the desk chair and tried to recall what it was like to be twenty-six. It was fun. What the hell was she doing with Brad? He was no fun. The last thing I wanted at twenty-six was a married father of two. Unless Dharma was counting on Brad soon being a divorced father of two, but that couldn't happen. At least not the way it was probably playing out in her head.

I had twenty more minutes before I had to leave to pick up the kids from school. I used it to find and print out his company's sexual harassment policy. I put it in a folder and filed it next to the dental insurance folder in Brad's cabinet. I knew he'd never find it, but I didn't care if he did. It was only a matter of time now.

JENNA WALKED IN MY SIDE door as if she lived with me. Her children ran past her and up the stairs to find mine in their rooms. "So what's so important that you summoned me over here on a weeknight?"

Nights like this, I wished Jenna could still drink. We would have drunk our way through this nightmare. Instead, I poured us each a cup of green tea. I blew into the scorching water, recognizing this was my last chance to turn back. The last moment before I shared a secret that could not be unsaid.

"Brad has a girlfriend, and I'm going to leave him."

Jenna turned her head to the side and placed her steaming cup on the counter. "Huh?" she asked as she tried to get a better handle on what I'd obviously already come to terms with.

"He's seeing someone." I paused to let that sink in. "She's twenty-six and she works for him."

Jenna's mouth fell open, but no words came out. Her silence was a bit daunting.

"As far as I can tell, they've been together for a while."

"Like, how long is a while? Are you sure?"

"I'm sure. He's having a difficult time managing her." Jenna's eyebrows shot up. "He's a bear to live with, and I think it's because she's pressuring him to leave me. Knowing my husband, he arrogantly assumed he could fuck this girl with no ramifications, but there are always consequences."

Jenna's face twisted in disgust. "What a fucking asshole."

"I know."

"How do you know, though?"

"I caught them in a heated argument at his holiday party in January, and I have gone through our phone records. She calls him constantly at all sorts of odd hours. Oh, and when he's drunk, he gets nasty and tells me he'll never lose me. Why would he say that unless he knew he should lose me?"

"What are you going to do? Are you going to move out? Do you need a place to stay?" Jenna never loved Brad, but this was beyond both our scopes of understanding.

"I'm not going anywhere. I just need Brad to agree to a few things he's not going to like. Like a divorce and giving me sole custody of James and Liv."

"Brad's going to be a total dick." She took a sip of her tea.

"I know. That's why I need your help."

"Anything. Do you want me to follow him?"

"No. I think his girlfriend will help us. We just need to piss her off enough."

Jenna observed me as if she were watching a documentary on a deranged killer. She was equally appalled and intrigued. "Who are you?"

"I'm Daniel, and my marriage is the lion's den."

❧

I FORCED THE ENDLESS THOUGHTS of Vince's hands touching me from my mind and focused on my husband. My goal was different now. I'd switched from trying to save our marriage to orchestrating the end of it.

"She's none of your fucking business," was what Brad had yelled at Dharma at the holiday party. He was talking about me, which meant I intrigued Dharma. Interested her enough to find me on Facebook and anywhere else she could locate information about me.

I did what any good wife would do. I unlocked my Instagram account and started posting frequently on that as well as Facebook. I would make it so I was her business. The very first picture went up on Valentine's Day. First thing in the morning, I posted our wedding portrait. He'd wanted that wedding. Something told me he wasn't going to be as excited about it when his girlfriend was faced with it. I knew exactly how she'd feel. I'd felt it myself the year before when I'd been jealous of Vince and his wife.

I made airtight plans with Brad. He promised Liv, James, and me that he'd be home on time. The kids were making us a romantic dinner. I knew he'd try to get out of it and that Dharma would flex her muscles—all of them—to keep him with her that night, but I was prepared.

Around lunchtime, I posted the second picture of us that Liv had taken at the shore when I was professing my love for her. I was leaning back on Brad and his arms were around me. The picture would infuriate Dharma.

"Hey," Brad answered his work phone in a rush. He didn't have time for my call. He was busy working.

"I just found a picture of the two of us under Liv's pillow," I lied. "I think this dinner means more to her than we could have imagined."

"Why the hell is that? It's going to be impossible to get out of here. And then the traffic." He was pathetic. Every time he opened his mouth, it became clearer that he didn't deserve any of us.

"I told Liv all of that. And she said she was going to pray to God that you'd be home on time." I could practically hear the sweat dripping from his brow. "We love you."

And at precisely four thirty P.M. on Valentine's Day, an exact replica of my wedding bouquet was delivered to Brad's office. The card read:

You are our everything.
We love you.

forty

LIKE ANY GOOD FRIEND WOULD do, Jenna suddenly became quite the participant on Facebook. A shutterbug, too. Every other weekend we met up with her and John somewhere, and Jenna would take our picture. She was the perfect partner in crime, always seeming nonchalant but not giving anyone a minute to refuse having their photo taken. Since I was always ready, the pictures came out fantastic and were the perfect representation of our love, which was an enormous feat because Brad was disgusting. I hid my hate for him while lots of people commented about what a beautiful couple we were. Their praise meant absolutely nothing to me.

I, of course, thanked everyone in a comment, knowing each time I did it showed up on more timelines. Jenna or I would post right after she took the picture, and then we'd watch as Brad suddenly had to excuse himself for what we knew was the tongue-lashing he was receiving through texts. In general, he was irritable, but after we started our campaign, he was downright wretched. I knew it was working because if he was miserable then that meant Dharma was, too.

I was banking on the fact that she was more of a gold-digger than just completely selfish and insane. She couldn't use his career to put pressure on him. That was what I planned to do. In order to force Brad to let me go, I needed leverage. Dharma was the only one who would give it to me. She'd realize I wasn't going anywhere. She'd come to me when he wouldn't leave me. I needed Dharma to crack, because I knew Brad never would. With every day that passed, my ability to stand the sight of him diminished, so she needed to snap sooner rather than later.

Brad was aging before my eyes. Drinking more and smoking cigars. He'd played both women wrong, and now, we were putting the screws to him, and he couldn't manage either of us.

I hoped.

MY OUTFIT WAS A HEAD-TURNER. It was unnecessary in every way, and yet completely perfect for my trip to my loving husband's office. It was a leather pencil skirt with a black turtleneck tucked in. The ensemble was actually subtle until your eyes fell to the four-and-a-half-inch spike heels I wore with it.

"Interesting outfit," Vince said as I dropped the files on the corner of his desk.

"This? It's nothing."

He leaned away from his desk and examined me from the top of my head to the stiletto heels I stood upon. "Nothing, huh?" His words were playful, yet his tone was filled with the heavy, unspoken lust that hung between us every day since I'd gone to the cabin.

"I need to leave a little early today." Vince only stared at me. I braved his silence without blinking. I wasn't a criminal he could force to speak.

When the silence became more uncomfortable than the flirting, he said, "I think that's a good idea," and broke into a smile. "I'm trying to concentrate here." Vince didn't know where I was going or what I was doing, but nothing had changed between us.

MY SOLE INTENTION WAS FOR everything to change between Brad and me. So, when I parked in the garage under his office building, I left my coat in the car. I was there to be seen.

By everyone. It was good to leave a lasting impression. Soon Brad and I would be done, and no one discussing our demise should ever have any excuse for his behavior. I wanted the witnesses to be properly appalled that he would ever cheat on his *beautiful* wife.

"Brad Walsh, please," I said to the receptionist, and then I added, "Let him know his wife is here." I turned away from her desk to hide the smile forming on my face. I was enjoying this too much. He deserved it, though. I rolled my eyes as I heard the security door open behind me.

"What are you doing here?" Brad was at ease. He kissed me on the cheek and appraised my outfit.

"I had lunch with Christine in the city and had to stop by and show you something."

"What?" He was confused. He was an idiot.

"I need to show you in your office."

"Now? We're kind of in the middle of something." The weasel I expected emerged. It was never far from the surface.

I leaned up and pressed my body against the front of him as I whispered in his ear, "It will only take a minute."

Brad sighed. I wasn't leaving. He held out his arm for me to lead the way and reached in front of me to press his badge against the security door lock. It opened, and I walked through the door of Brad's domain.

He was silent, almost sneaking me in, and then karma helped by bringing Amit out of his office at the exact moment we approached it.

"Meredith! What are you doing here?"

"I just stopped by to show Brad something," I said, making sure to sound as if what I wanted to show him was my nipple in his mouth.

Amit glanced down at my legs, smiled back at me, and then winked at Brad. "Goddamn, you are one lucky bastard, Brad." Amit was loud and boisterous. He was easy to love, a complete flirt, and always fun. Heads began to pop out of cubicles, and I could feel Dharma's presence by the stiffening of Brad's neck next to me.

"Let's go in my office." Brad rushed me along.

I hugged Amit one last time and followed Brad into his office. He shut the door behind me, and a slight sense of relief fell between us. "Now what did you have to show me?"

I lifted the turtleneck over my head, making sure to mess up my hair as I raised it. I took my time. I walked to the chair in front of his desk and draped it over the back. I knew Brad was looking at my ass even without turning around.

"Meredith?"

I walked to my husband and stroked his dick through his pants. Brad's eyes bulged. I stopped before he was completely hard. I unhooked my bra from the back and let it fall to the floor as I held my forearm across my nipples. I turned and displayed my side to him. A small infinity symbol was tattooed there, right on my ribs.

"What the hell is that?" Brad forgot where he was and who he was hiding from.

"It's a tattoo. An infinity symbol." I moved my hand farther to the side and then completely let it drop, exposing both my breasts. Brad's eyes darted from the tattoo, to my nipples, and back again.

"I can see that." He leaned down, examining the tattoo, and I let my fingers caress my nipple closest to his face.

"Do you like it?"

"Yeah." He shook his head, still in disbelief. "I love it." His breath was hot on my skin. "It's sexy as fuck." Brad stood up, and I unzipped his pants and released him.

I pushed him back to his desk and pulled his pants down. The idea of his dick anywhere near me made me sick, but some things were necessary.

"Since when did you want a tattoo?"

Brad sat on his desk, and I stroked him harder, praying he could come without touching the inside of me. "It reminds me of you." *And how our love is nothing of the sort. It has a very finite end point.* I let my hot breath caress his ear and took his lobe in my mouth, moaning.

"Fuck, Meredith, I'm going to come."

"You should. Come, Brad."

He dropped his head back and lifted his shirt before coming all over his stomach.

I released him and waited for his breathing to return to normal. "Well, I won't keep you. I have to get back for carpool," I said, and Brad grabbed a tissue from his desk to clean his stomach and pulled his pants up.

"It's hot, Meredith." He gathered me into his arms and kissed me. My insides turned at the prospects of where his lips had been. He held me close and his hands ran through my already tousled hair. His breath was heavy when he finally released me.

"I'm glad you like it."

I redressed in my bra and turtleneck, only tucking in half of my top. I pretended to smooth down my hair, and I grabbed my purse before opening the door to Brad's office. Dharma was leaning into a cubicle ten feet away. She straightened as she saw me, and I smiled, having recognized her from the holiday party and having just sent the message that her boyfriend was still fucking his wife. I waved to her and turned to smile at Brad one last time before I walked out.

Brad didn't come home until after ten that night. He was exhausted.

forty-one

"CAN I TALK TO YOU a minute?" I asked Vince as soon as I got to work, as if the answer would ever be no.

He stopped pouring his coffee. "Of course," Vince said and then paused to look at me.

Things had settled into a serene calm between us. Vince kept his distance. We stayed professional and away from personal topics, and I continued to dream about him. I grabbed a tablet and closed his office door as I walked through it. Vince sat rigid in his chair, his light demeanor gone.

"What's wrong?" I asked.

"Are you going to tell me you're quitting?"

"No. Not yet." *Not ever, I hope.* "I need to talk to you about security for the spring fair at the elementary school." Vince laughed and leaned back in his chair. "Apparently, the sex was so good with you I actually lost my mind and started volunteering to chair horrible committees."

"It was that good."

Our laughter trailed off and was replaced by a deep need suspended between us. I couldn't breathe.

I might have needed mouth-to-mouth.

I cleared my throat. "So, what's going on with you? Are you seeing anyone?" I joked, but the assumption that he'd wait for me was ridiculous. I wasn't the only person in this town dreaming of Vincent Pratt. Jenna had already informed me that every woman was talking about our very hot, and recently single, chief of police. They were shameless. But even if Vince moved on, I'd still love him forever.

"No." Lost in my own depressing thoughts, I had forgotten what I'd asked him. I looked at Vince, confused. "I'm not seeing anyone." A deep sigh took over my confusion. "Why? Do you want to see me?" *God, I would love to.* "Naked?" he added in with a slight smile on his lips.

"Is this how the spring fair security meeting usually goes?"

"No." Vince shook his head and never took his eyes off me.

"How come you never tell me I'm beautiful?" In all the time we'd spent together, with and without our clothes on, he'd never used the worn-out "beautiful" compliment.

"You are."

"But you never tell me."

"Because I don't think you consider it a compliment. You prefer to be utilized rather than idolized."

"Why are you so different today?" There wasn't an ounce of displeasure in my voice. I'd missed him flirting with me more than I let myself realize. "So forward?"

"I've been on Facebook."

"I thought I suggested you stay off there."

"You did." He nodded, still smiling. "And I behaved for a while, but I couldn't help myself. You post so often now that it's as if you're trying to communicate with someone."

"Facebook is designed to connect people."

"It seems like you're trying to connect with new people." He was taunting me, chiding me into telling him what was going on. Vince turned to his computer and pulled up my Facebook profile. He scrolled through my pictures and clicked on one of Brad sitting on a barstool, with me draped over him, kissing his cheek. "I know you, Meredith. You'd never post a picture like this unless you were up to something."

"Me?" I raised my hands to my chest. "I just thought it was

time to start sharing more with the world."

"Has Brad noticed? Because he knows you pretty well, too."

"I don't think so. He's been so busy. What with work and all."

"Of course." Vince's face turned dark. "Be careful." He stared right into my eyes. "You're playing with fire." He looked back at the picture on his screen and then shut the window on his computer. When he turned back, his playful demeanor was gone. I was hurting him, and I hated it. I wanted to step behind his desk and fall into his lap. I wanted to kneel between his knees and take him in my mouth. I would have climbed into his truck and raced to his cabin.

"Vince—"

"It's okay." He stood, and I rose to my feet. I needed to get out of his office. I needed some distance. "I know this is what it is for now. We're friends, and if it's the only way I can have you, then I'll take it." He took a deep breath. "It's just nearly impossible not to love you." His words sank down between us. I loved him, too.

"I can quit. You won't have to see me every day." The idea tore my heart from my chest. I needed to be near him every waking moment. I'd convinced myself it was enough just to be in his presence. Quitting my job would be yet another layer of misery, but I wouldn't spend my days hurting Vince.

"No. I don't want you to leave."

I owed him so much more than I could give him while I was still with Brad. I wouldn't have another affair. I took two steps toward him and selfishly laid my hands flat on his stomach. The fabric of his uniform was rough under my palms. He watched as I slid them up to his chest. "I'm going to be honest."

"Always."

"Deadly so," I said, and Vince finally looked from my hands to my face. "I've been thinking. A lot. Pretty much every hour I'm awake, I am trying to figure out what happened last year.

What would have made me cheat on my family the way I did."
I felt him tense beneath my hands. His chest rose as he breathed
in my dismissal of our love. "I was unhappy—horribly unhappy—and lonely. I let you fix what you never broke. I let you fill a
spot you never vacated. I slipped into the darkness, because I'd
follow you to hell if you asked me to."

Vince placed his hands over mine on his chest. He moved
them close to his heart. "I won't apologize to anyone about last
year."

"You'll never have to apologize to me for it, but I can't live
in the dark anymore. I want to have a real life."

Vince took my hands in his own, and his warmth filled me
like soft candlelight in a dark room. The heat became unbearable, sticking my clothes and my hair to my skin.

"If I were to tell you the truth right now," my voice cracked
a little as I spoke. "I would tell you that I love you, and I want to
be with you every moment of the day."

Vince lowered his head, and I pulled it to my shoulder. We
were becoming champions of impossible situations. I tightened
my arms around his neck and inhaled him, letting him fill me,
because even just that was enough.

I stepped back from him and steadied myself. "I need to talk
to you about security for the spring fair."

"You are relentless," he said, finally laughing.

"You hope."

forty-two

HOW LONG? HOW LONG WAS this whole thing going to go on? It'd been five weeks already and besides watching Brad's misery increase, nothing had come out of it. Brad had left for Singapore, so I wouldn't have any new pictures to post online. I wasn't sure if Dharma was with him, and I wasn't willing to stake out her apartment to find out.

"Allison said I'm invited to her birthday party," Liv said as I put her lunchbox in her backpack. We'd been in the new house less than a week, and the three of us were already feeling like we were home. There were constant construction crews still there, but the bulk of the work was done.

"That's nice. Allison Pratt?"

"Yes. The colonel's daughter."

"I know who you mean."

"Aren't her parents getting divorced?" James said, and both Liv and I turned to him in shock. It was completely unlike James to talk about anything personal about himself or anyone else.

"Who told you that?" I asked, and James shook his head. I took the clean bowls out of the dishwasher and placed them in the cabinet.

"They are divorced," Liv said. She barely looked up from her cereal bowl. "Mommy, why do people get divorced?"

I stopped everything I was doing. "I don't know why

Allison's parents got divorced. I don't know why anyone gets divorced. It's something very personal between a husband and a wife."

"And their children," James added.

"The divorce changes children's lives forever, but the causes are always about the parents." I paused and made sure both of my children were listening. "It's hard to explain, but the love a mommy and daddy have for each other is different than the love they have for their children. There is no such thing as divorce when it comes to a parent and their child. It is absolutely impossible for a mommy to stop loving her son or daughter."

"It's an infinite love," James said.

"Yes. It goes on forever."

"If you and Dad get divorced, are you going to move away?" Liv asked.

"Never," I answered too quickly, and then regretted it. I had no guarantees about the future. "Wherever you guys are is where I'll be. I would be horribly lonely without you."

"True, probably Dad will move away. He's used to not seeing us."

"You know, even when Daddy is away, he loves you just as much?"

"I know."

❧

I DROPPED THE KIDS OFF at school and drove to the police station. Why did life have to be so hard? Vince was drinking a cup of coffee and reading some reports when I went in. I wanted to lay down with him, again. I walked toward his door. I was about to turn away, the same way I had the previous days before, but I paused. I was torn. I needed to be away from him for my sanity and near him for my happiness. There must be something between crazy and happy. That was my marriage, though.

"Hey, I heard Allison's party is coming up."

"Olivia invited?"

"Yes. Any idea what she wants? We need to go this weekend and buy her a present."

"The only thing she asked for was for me to move back in."

My heart sank as I watched the sadness fall across Vince's face. "Oh, Vince." He didn't say a word to make it better. There was nothing he could say. "Did you think about it?"

What is coming out of my mouth?

I held up my hand before he could answer, "Don't answer that."

"It's okay. I did think about it. I thought about how Lynn and I could make it work and let our kids have their lives back."

"And?"

"And there's just no way. Even before I left, there was no way, but now too much has happened. Lynn is happy. I'm happy."

"You both just have to keep working hard to make sure your kids are happy."

"I know."

"You're an amazing father." Vince didn't say anything. He just looked at me as if he'd been through a war, and in a way, he had been. "You're an incredible person." He smiled a little. I was breaking through. "You're a phenomenal lover."

We heard steps behind us as Thompson came through the front entrance of the barracks, whistling. I turned around and returned to my desk. If there was such a thing as the right way to handle the end of a marriage, Vince was doing it. He was respectful, loving, and kind. And to Lynn's knowledge—and my own at the moment—there was no one else involved. His children were his priority.

Then there was Brad and me. We deserved each other. Cheating, lying, conniving. Vince was too good to be in the same town as us, let alone wrapped up in our nonsense. I was spending my time trying to get Brad's little whore to deliver the evidence I needed to extort a divorce from him. Posting pictures and quotes online to enrage her to the point of show-ing up with screenshots of texts from Brad's phone professing his love for her. Pictures, too, I hoped. I'd staple copies of all of them to Brad's corporate sexual harassment policy, along with a divorce agreement that gave me sole custody. I'd threaten to expose Brad to the executive board of his firm if he didn't sign. I would do anything to keep my kids.

I wallowed in these ideas the rest of the day. Vince went out on patrol, and I lingered in his office while I dropped off the files I'd completed. His wedding picture was missing. What do you do with your wedding portrait after a marriage ends and you take it down?

I'd gone from being not the kind of woman who had an affair, to the kind of woman who taunted her husband's lover over the Internet. I needed to reevaluate myself and my situa-tion, because as good of a man as Vince was, I was unimpressed with myself.

I left the office and drove to the kids' school. I waited in the carpool line and tried to convince myself Brad was the reason I was a terrible person. If there were a chance he could be civil, I wouldn't be in this situation. I snaked through the line, waited for Liv and James's names to be called.

By the time I was close to the front, I let myself off the hook. I wanted to talk to Vince about it. He would make me feel better. He would tell me I wasn't as terrible as I thought I was, but I couldn't. I had to stay away from him. For both of our sakes.

James climbed in the car first and dove over the back seat into the third row. Liv followed and buckled up behind me. We drove through our little town as the clouds floated by above us. And then Liv said, "Sometimes I just feel like this is all someone else's dream, and I'm just a part of it."

"I know what you mean," I said.

Or a nightmare.

forty-three

BRAD HAD BEEN IN SINGAPORE for three weeks. It felt like six months. I took the time off from Facebook and just lived my real life the entire time. Liv, James, and I attended church every Sunday. They went to Sunday school and learned about God's love and Jesus. I sat alone and watched the colonel. I had too much to confess to really pay attention to the sermons. If I listened to them, I might actually regret my latest endeavor, which was quickly becoming a burden. Torturing people was exhausting. Plus, there was always a chance my assumptions about Dharma's motivations were completely wrong, however unlikely that may be.

When Brad returned, I promised myself I'd keep up the social media assault until the end of April. It was only two weeks away, and if nothing came of it, I had to come up with another plan. I wasn't doing Brad *or* the swim team over the summer break. Maybe this was karma. Maybe I deserved to live the rest of my life watching Brad fuck his young whore. That wasn't nice. I was banking on her not being a whore and that she was somehow in love with Brad. God bless her.

NEW DRESS. NEW MAKEUP. NEW shoes. Same drill, except on this particular Saturday, Brad and I spent the day with a real estate agent, looking at two condos in the city. Brad hated the first one, but the second condo impressed him to the point of wanting to put in an offer immediately. It was a two-bedroom co-op in a great neighborhood. It surprised me that Brad was more interested in high-end fixtures and unique architecture than a doorman and a twenty-four-hour fitness center.

After we parted ways with the realtor, I surprised him with dinner reservations at a restaurant a block from Dharma's apartment. He was difficult at first, but he eventually caved and drove us to the restaurant.

Had they eaten here before?

Maybe. I didn't care. Caring wasn't part of my plan.

Brad ordered a bottle of cabernet as soon as we were seated at a small table by the windows. He was the old Brad, happy something had been decided. He was a deal closer. I sipped my wine and checked in on Facebook while Brad discussed an offer with the realtor on his phone. The other patrons began to stare, and he stood and walked out the front door of the restaurant.

I could see through the window that Brad was nodding and smiling as he spoke into the phone. The condo had been on the market one hundred twenty-seven days. There should be no counter offers. Brad continued to speak and nod. He was shaking his head, and then he tilted his face to the sky. It was taking so long, I wasn't sure if he was still on the phone with the realtor, but then he turned and walked back into the restaurant. He'd lost his jolly demeanor. The constant stress that surrounded Brad Walsh returned.

We ate our lobster raviolis in silence. When Brad looked up, I smiled at him to put him at ease, but sweat covered his forehead. If something didn't give, he was going to have a heart attack.

"Did you notice where the bathroom was when you went outside?" I asked

"It's just past the hostess stand. On the left," Brad said and finished his glass of wine. While he refilled it, I stood and grabbed my purse from the back of my chair and walked away.

The bathroom was small. It had two occupied stalls and wallpaper with large white roses covering the non-square walls. The giant roses had dark green leaves between them, making the immense pattern feel as if it were everywhere around me, even above my head. I was drowning in the white roses. Both stalls freed at the same time, and I slipped into one. I listened as the women talked about the out-of-date wallpaper and the sloping floors while they washed their hands. And then I was alone with my mind. The frustration with my marriage was spilling over in my head. It was time to talk to Brad. To try honesty.

The notion consumed me. I almost convinced myself Brad could be civil if we split up. I washed my hands, lost in the idea that we could co-parent Liv and James without any hatred or regret. As I pulled the lever on the paper towel holder, I decided tonight was the night Brad and I would talk. I inhaled deeply and slowly exhaled.

We can do this.

The door opened, and Dharma walked in.

She looked like hell. Her tight, boob-highlighting dress from the party was replaced with yoga pants and a stained Key West T-shirt. Her eyes were swollen, as if she hadn't slept the night before or was having some type of allergic reaction.

A lump lodged in my throat. I'd imagined this conversation a hundred times in my mind, and Dharma had always looked exactly the same as she had at the party—stunning, with her boobs in everyone's face. I was losing my edge. She suddenly seemed very young. But her youth was my ally.

"Hello," I said. The word was slow to form, and even slower to be said.

"Do you remember me? I'm Dharma."

"Yes. From the office party. How are you?"

Like an animal caught in a cage, Dharma's eyes darted around the room. I stayed perfectly still, and eventually,
Dharma's scrutiny settled on me. She was fidgeting and obviously on edge. Like, maybe the edge of reason. "I need to talk
to you." She locked the outside door of the restroom before
turning back to face me. Dharma was petite. I had at least four
inches on her. I could use the heel of my shoe as a weapon if I
had to.

"Sure," I said and checked my purse for my phone. This was
not going as planned. "What's on your mind?"

"Your husband has been cheating on you for two years."

Two years.

Shock held my breath and forced me to look Dharma over
again. I calculated back. Back before Vince, before I'd hated or
loved my town. Disgust for my husband and his whore standing
in front of me stole every logical thought I had.

"How do you know that?" I asked.

Dharma was completely unfazed. As if she was respond-
ing to a form e-mail. "Because he's in love with me." Even this
statement wasn't filled with the buoyant arrogance of youth. It
was anchored by depression.

"Do you love him?" I needed her to love him to rid myself
of him.

"I would do anything for him." The words slipped from her
lips as if she'd spoken them a hundred times before. My skin
tingled with the realization that this woman had been between
my husband and me for years.

"But do you love him? You seem too young to be involved in
someone else's marriage."

Dharma stared behind me, and I turned to see what was
there. There was nothing but the overbearing wallpaper. I
turned back, and she was still entranced by the horrible white
roses. In her empty eyes, I realized what was scaring me.
Something was different about Dharma. The fight was gone,

and it had been replaced by nothing.

"I'm not too young." She rummaged through the bag hanging across her chest and pulled out a gun. The muscles in the back of my neck tightened, lifting my head and straightening my spine. I told myself to breathe.

"Of course not," I said and kept my voice steady.

"You don't believe me?" Dharma peered down at the gun as she voiced the words.

"It's not that I don't believe you," I rushed out. I wanted her to be calm, so I slowed my words down. "It's just a lot to take in."

"He was always with me," she said, and for the life of me, I had no idea how to react, or even how she wanted me to react. So, I said nothing and hoped that wouldn't piss her off. "Every time he told you he was at a business dinner or a *team building* event." She dramatically waved the gun in the air communicating she was not happy with my reaction. "He was with *me*."

"Really?" was all I could force from my lips. The gun held my attention and left me speechless. Until a tiny voice in my head said, "He must have had some business dinners," and I was proud of myself for remaining silent.

"He likes the way I fuck him." This little bitch was going to lock me in a bathroom and tell me how my husband liked to be fucked. "He likes that I'm adventurous."

Adventurous, or a slut?

I took a step toward the door, and Dharma blocked me. Her makeup looked like it was left over from the night before and she smelled of stale liquor. Brad and she deserved each other. I couldn't stand the sight of either of them.

"I'm going to go." For a split second, I thought she might let me pass. There was something so absent about her.

"He loves me," she said again, and I stopped breathing. "I have proof. I have proof that he loves me." She held the gun in her right hand and pulled her phone out with her other. She used her middle finger to swipe through items on the screen, the gun swinging in her hand as she moved it. She paused at something and a slow, horrible laugh shook her chest as she glared at me. "Look at this."

Dharma stepped closer. She handed me the phone, but I didn't take it. She rolled her eyes at me and held the phone up in front of my face. It was a video with the white triangle in the middle waiting to be pressed. Dharma used her gun hand to press it, and the video began to play while we both watched.

It was Dharma, sitting on a couch wearing only a garter belt and touching herself. I winced and tilted my face away from her phone.

She pointed the gun at my head and said, "Keep watching."

I turned back as the wine in my stomach churned and threatened to come up. A man came and kneeled in front of Dharma on the screen and began having sex with her. I couldn't see his face, but I knew it was Brad. I knew by the width of his shoulders, his naked ass, and the perfectly cut hair on the back of his head. The video repulsed me. How could he have had sex with this *girl*? Made a movie? Anger at both of them settled me. Dharma assumed she could come interrupt my dinner with her little show, and I would just disappear. She was a child with no idea of who I was. She'd only had Brad's opinion to go on, and he didn't know me either.

"Now do you believe that he loves me?" Dharma was smiling, but her expression was joyless.

With the gun to my head, I said, "That only proves that he fucked you."

Immediately, I regretted the words leaving my mouth.

Dharma pressed the gun barrel to her temple and pulled the trigger, splattering blood all over the white roses on the wall behind her. I stood still and watched the blood run on the floor around her head, and my thoughts and emotions left me. Possibly forever. I no longer deserved to feel things in this life.

I didn't even jump at the noise. As if I knew it was coming. I knew it was going to be her and not me, and yet I still couldn't let her think he loved her.

Maybe he did love her.

Maybe he wasn't capable of love.

The knob on the door turned violently, and the silence in the room was replaced by the pounding against the wood door. It was forced open by the same waiter who'd filled my wine glass when we'd first arrived. He stopped abruptly at the sight of Dharma lying on the floor at my feet. She was on her side, her feet behind her knees. The gun was next to her. The blood was everywhere.

"She shot herself," I said and waited for him to do something. I stood perfectly still, wishing the waiter could put me on a tray and carry me back to my table. Back to my husband who was as despicable as I was.

"Meredith!" Brad rushed into the bathroom and was pushed out by the waiter, who was yelling at the hostess to call 9-1-1.

forty-four

I BECAME THE WITNESS TO the end of Dharma's life. I was placed on a barstool until the police arrived. There was an ambulance, but Dharma was already gone. I'd been there when she'd left. I was the last person she'd spoken to, the last one to hear her sad story.

It was easy to remain brief. There wasn't much of me left. I stayed close to the truth. I was using the restroom, and she came in. She locked the door and pulled out a gun. She made me watch a video of her and a man having sex, and then she shot herself. It was all very bizarre.

My hands were swabbed for gunshot residue. It was procedure. My information was taken down, and I was offered a ride to the hospital, but I wanted to go home. I needed to see Liv and James. They would save me from whatever *this* was.

Brad practically carried me to his car. He was compassionate and kind, and no longer seemed to be trapped in a vise. When he opened the car door for me, he held me tight against his chest and whispered in my ear, "I couldn't lose you."

BRAD PAID THE BABYSITTER, AND we put the kids to bed. They were exhausted, it was already well past their bedtime. I changed out of my beautiful dress, the one I'd worn to torment Brad's young girlfriend that now had her blood splattered on the skirt. Brad was opening more wine when I entered the kitchen. Without a word, I lifted the glass to my lips with a shaking hand.

"Are you okay?" he asked, but nothing was ever going to be okay again.

"I'm in shock."

"Do you want to talk about it?" he asked, and he wasn't angry. He wasn't being a dick.

"I want to talk about *all* of it." Brad lowered his eyes in shame. "About Dharma and you and me, and how the hell we ended up here."

"Would you believe me if I told you she never meant a thing to me?"

I longed for the time I'd felt nothing for Brad. Now, the sight of him evoked the urge to throw something at him. I couldn't be far enough away from him. He actually repelled me. "Of course I would." His head hung low toward the counter. "If you weren't such a disgusting liar."

Brad's eyes met mine. They were tired and kind, and for some reason, I smiled. I was in shock and unable to control or predict my reactions. "Do you think they're going to connect me to her?" He was a coward.

"I don't think they'll investigate much further. Suicide's not a crime. It's a tragedy." Brad took another sip of his wine. "I guess there's always a chance of a civil suit. Or some consequences at your office. Is there any evidence of your and Dharma's—" I could barely say it. I hated him. I wished I'd never met him. "Relationship?"

Brad shook his head defiantly. "No. No pictures. No notes. No cards."

"I saw the video. I know it was you. I'm guessing that wasn't the first time you were an idiot."

Brad took another sip of his wine. How could he drink? How could he live with himself? His mouth twisted in disgust.

He didn't like being caught. "You couldn't see my face. There were some texts. And one of her friend's joined us once." I let the hatred linger in my glare. "A few times."

"You're quite the ladies' man."

"Don't be an asshole."

"Right, I'm the asshole."

Brad shook his head and drank more wine.

"How did this happen?" I asked.

"I don't know."

I needed to know. "Why don't we try being honest . . . just this once."

"Fine. Let's start with you. When did you find out about her? Because I sure as fuck know you didn't just all of a sudden enjoy sharing our *love* on Facebook."

"That little scene at the holiday party told me everything I needed to know. Although Liv picked up on it when she went to your office. So I'm guessing if an eight-year-old could figure it out, one of your adept coworkers was probably able to decipher the subtleties as well."

"So you *were* fucking with her on Facebook?"

"I didn't hate Dharma." I yelled at the idiot I'd married. "At least, I didn't think so until I saw that video." The anger tried to break through my numbed mind, but I was through with emotions. "Then I realized I wasn't as ready to be replaced as I'd thought."

"Does that mean you're staying?" Brad was quiet, mild again.

"Not a chance. Why were you fucking her in the first place?"

Brad stood up straight, and I braced myself for his words. "Because when we moved here, I thought we were going to live happily ever after. That I would work, you would take care of the house and the kids, and we would ride off into the sunset." Brad walked around the counter and stood in front of me. "But every day that we were here, you withered away a little more

217

and hated me in the process."

"I was so alone here. You'd come home from work smelling of beer and reeking of pride and satisfaction, and I had throw up in my hair." Brad rolled his eyes, still not caring what I was saying. "I was isolated." Brad looked away, dismissing my words as usual. "But I never felt as alone as when I was standing next to you."

"I couldn't make you love it here. I couldn't even get you to like it here," he said, and I felt his frustration. On my own, I couldn't make myself love it here either.

"So how does that equate to you fucking a twenty-six-year-old at your office?"

"She didn't hate me." That should have been his first hint she was unstable. I could have screamed at him that he was pathetic, but the conversation was already filled with hypocrisy. "Meredith—"

"I'm going to bed."

Brad placed his glass on the island and pulled me to his chest. It was as if he'd never hugged me before. The familiarity of his body was gone. He wasn't the man I'd walked down the aisle to. He wasn't the man who'd saved me in a bar the first night he spoke to me.

"Alone. I want to go to bed alone."

He held me at arm's length and searched my eyes for some shred of kindness toward him, but I hated us both. "Mer, we'll get through this. We'll have a fresh start."

"You are insane. I'm never going to get through this, and we are completely done."

He stepped back. "You'll feel better in the morning. Go. Get some sleep."

Brad didn't care about a word I'd said.

forty-five

I WAS STILL LYING AWAKE in my bed, alone and distraught, when Brad walked into the room shortly after sunrise.

"I want us to go to church today."

"I'm done with what you want," I said and rolled back toward the window. I felt each of his footsteps as he walked across the room. He sat on the edge of my bed, touching me. A chill slid over my skin where his arm rested. Repulsion followed in its wake. He rolled me onto my back and leaned over my waist, facing me.

"I know you're angry."

I raised my eyebrows.

"And probably a million other things, but we have to pull this together for James and Liv."

His words met me one at a time. I couldn't process them any faster. I was physically and emotionally exhausted, and all I wanted to do was lay in my bed and sleep, but sleep wouldn't come. Dharma had taken it with her when she'd shot herself, and like her, I feared sleep was never coming back.

I sat up and leaned back against our headboard. "Okay. I'll shower."

❧

BRAD MADE US BREAKFAST. THE kids chatted and debated as if their father's lover hadn't put a bullet in her head in front

219

of me. I wanted to scream at them to shut up, but that would let the disgustingness of my marriage affect their lives, and I would do whatever I could to avoid that.

I was right about everything. I was a *Dateline* episode. I was the town scandal. I was a whore—even if no one else knew it but the colonel and me. The thought of him made me cry. I stood in the center of my closet, looking for something to wear to church and crying because I was in love with a man I would never be worthy of. He deserved so much better than me.

"Hurry up." Brad's voice was soft. He was tender, the way he'd been when my father had died. Brad was going to take care of me. "Hey. Are you crying?" He stepped into my closet and tilted my head up to face him. I dropped it to his chest and cried some more. "Shh. I promise we're going to get through this."

"I don't want to get through this," I said, and I wasn't sure what I meant, but I wasn't going to let him make it all better. I should have to wallow in it. I deserved to suffer. She wasn't even thirty, for God's sake, and she'd taken her own life because she'd been involved with us.

"Meredith. You didn't do this to her. She did it to herself."

"Please, stop talking." I moved away from Brad, slipped a jersey dress over my head, and spotted the dress I'd worn to Brad's holiday party. It was hanging on a hook on the wall, safe in its dry cleaning bag, and I wanted to burn it. I wanted to erase every memory of Dharma. I looked at Brad. Disgust filled my soul. How could he move? How could he speak? Did she mean nothing to him?

"Mommy, I'm ready." Liv with her blue-streaked hair bounced into my closet. She was wearing a summer dress with suede boots and a down coat more suitable for cold weather. Something wasn't right about her outfit. Everything was wrong with her mother.

"Is it warm enough for that dress?"

"It's really hot out," Liv said, and I questioned whether I'd ever comprehend the weather again.

"Well, you look beautiful," I lied.

❧

WE WALKED INTO CHURCH AS a family. We were the biggest lie to ever walk through the door. Brad's phone was silent. There was no one left to text him. We signed the kids into Sunday school and found the only two seats left in the sanctuary. They were on the aisle, about five rows from the front. I lowered my head and begged my mind to stay silent. Why couldn't I lose my memory today?

Brad took my hand and held it on his lap. I let him. I didn't have the strength to fight with him, and frankly I didn't care. I hadn't cared about him touching me in years. I glanced up— right into the eyes of Vincent Pratt. He, his oldest son, and Lynn were walking through the aisle, searching for seats. He was staring at my hand, and when he finally looked at me, his eyes were filled with questions. I had no explanation. I had no secret gesture or tiny smile. I was empty like Dharma's eyes the night before.

The colonel's family kept walking. They probably found seats behind us, but I didn't turn around to see where. I didn't care where he was either. I didn't care where any of us were. The sermon began. The pastor talked about finding time for the relationships in our lives that mattered and Brad squeezed my hand in his. We sang. We prayed. Brad dropped an envelope in the offering basket, and then we collected Liv and James and left.

We walked out into the glaring sunshine and the heat of the first warm day of the year. I squinted and searched through my purse for my sunglasses. It was too bright out. A young girl had taken her own life last night. She'd spent the day walking and talking. She'd put a gun in her bag and had gone to a restaurant, and then I'd said something and she'd pointed the gun at her head and killed herself. How could it be so fucking sunny?

Brad drove us home, and we spent the day with our kids. They were delighted their parents were playing with them. Soccer, tennis, board games, we did it all. Liv commented at dinner that it had been her favorite day so far, and Brad looked at me, hopeful that this was a fresh start.

He was a monster. He'd forgotten about Dharma faster than she'd pulled the trigger.

forty-six

I'D SEEN DHARMA'S STORY ON the news one time. One lousy time it was mentioned that a woman had taken her own life in a trendy Italian restaurant in Center City. It was replaced by other tragic headlines before the next day, as if no one in the world except me was willing to take a minute out of their schedules to acknowledge the fact that she was gone. That she'd ever been here in the first place.

Monday morning, I said good-bye to Brad and dropped the kids off at school. I drove to the police station and the job that had made me fall in love with this town. Or was it the colonel? I parked next to his truck, but I couldn't go in. I couldn't face him. He was too good.

I put my car in drive and headed east toward the shore. I lost track of the roads and the time, and before I knew it, I was parking on a side street at The Point. I had my purse, my wedges, and the black shirtdress I'd put on that morning. I didn't care. I just needed to hear the ocean.

I locked the Escalade and climbed over the dune. It was windy. The soft sand swirled on the top of the beach and blew my hair into my eyes. The tiny particles pelting me were like sandpaper dragging across my skin, and I deserved it. The ocean would force me to feel something. It wouldn't let me just be.

I turned my back to the wind and watched the gray surf

pound against the sand. It was a violent day at the shore. My father and I would have worshipped the sea from the safety of the beach—we wouldn't have gone in the water when it was in that much turmoil. I missed him. I missed who I was when he was alive. I lay down with my back on the soft sand and my feet resting above me on the dune fence. I shielded myself from the wind and let the sound of the waves heal me.

THE SLEEP THAT HAD ESCAPED me the prior two nights finally took me with it. I dreamed I was in the ocean, alone but not lonely. I floated over the waves with the summer sun pouring over me and the silence of the water surrounding me. I was at peace, but the calm within me was pulled out with the tide.

When I woke up, the sand had covered half my body. If I lay here long enough, I'd be completely buried. I squinted and shielded my eyes from the sun. And then I felt him next to me.

Vince was leaning back against the fence. He was wearing his uniform and a look of deep concern. I didn't say hello. I didn't smile. I just stayed still beside him.

"You didn't come to work today." I hadn't called or even bothered to tell anyone where I was. Vince was the only person who cared. "I got Brad's number from Jenna and called him. He didn't know where you were." Vince rested his elbows on his knees and raised his fisted hands to his chin. "He said you'd had a rough weekend, but he wouldn't tell me anything else." I stayed silent, not sure of what to say. "Did I ever tell you that I hate your husband?"

I looked down and tried to hide. I wanted desperately to escape his eyes and I didn't want him to see what was hiding in my own. "No. You never told me that."

"What's going on?"

I inhaled deeply. The mix of Vince and the salt air was perfection. I wanted to walk into the ocean with him and swim away from here. I sat up and faced him. "Brad's girlfriend shot herself Saturday night." Vince had no reaction. I'd forgotten how good he was at this. "She locked me in a bathroom with her, made me watch a video of Brad fucking her, and then she shot herself."

"Oh my God. Are you all right?" Vince pulled me onto his lap and ran his hands down my arms and over my legs, checking for any signs of injury, but they were all hidden in my mind.

"She didn't hurt me," I said and moved away, settling back onto the soft sand. "She had the gun pointed at my head. She wanted me to know that Brad *loved* her, and I couldn't let her think it. I couldn't let her win. I told her he was only fucking her, and then she shot herself instead of me."

"You could have been killed."

I stayed still, unfazed by his concern and trapped in his stare.

Vince studied me. His eyes ran over every inch of me and then met my own again. I didn't look away. I didn't care. He already knew every horrible piece of me better than I knew myself. "You have this incredible ability to take responsibility for everything and everyone else. You can't fix the entire world." I looked away. "And you can't blame yourself."

I disagreed. "There is always someone to blame." The waves were louder, closing in with the coming tide, and the wind whipped the sea spray up on the dune. I closed my eyes and let the mist hit my face.

"So now what?" He could feel my distance, and now, he wanted answers I didn't have to give.

"I don't know."

"I saw you in church yesterday."

I lowered my head. I was even ashamed of that. I didn't deserve to go anywhere.

"Are you still hell-bent on not leaving your husband? Out of some convoluted, self-condemnation, are you actually considering *staying* with him?"

"I don't know what I'm doing."

Vince was hurt. I could see it in his eyes. I'd left him, and he knew it.

"Everything I've already done has been wrong." I grabbed a handful of sand and let it cascade down through my fingers. The wind caught it before it hit the ground, and it blew toward me. "I don't want to make any more decisions." I smoothed the sand beside me and then looked up at Vince. "I'm clearly horrible at it. You were right. I was playing with fire." A lump lodged in my throat.

"She had a gun and locked you in a bathroom. You put some pictures online."

I turned away from him and let the wind hit me in the face again. When I couldn't take it anymore, I ducked back to the shelter of the dune.

"You didn't kill her, Meredith. You didn't even know about her until a few months ago."

"Why couldn't I just keep my mouth shut?" I was disgusted with myself, and I was no better than my husband.

"And what? Let her kill you instead? You didn't put the gun in her purse, and you didn't point it at her head. Everyone has a choice, and just because you posted some pictures online, she wasn't forced to look at them. She was an adult who made her own choices.

"Vince held out his hand to me. "Come here." I shook my head and held back the tears. "Come here," he repeated, and I crawled over to him and laid my head on his shoulder. I wrapped my arm around his chest and I rested there, once again letting Vincent Pratt fix something he didn't break.

He didn't tell me everything was going to be all right. He didn't tell me not to worry about it or that we'd have a fresh start. He only said, "I love you," and it meant the world to me.

"I know," I said and somehow moved even closer to him. I closed my eyes and cried on Vince's shoulder.

"And when you need me, I'll be here."

"I know."

But the best thing I could do for Vince was stay the hell away from him.

forty-seven

BRAD WAS NEARLY BACK TO his old self. He was funny and pleasant without the constant stress of Dharma to deal with. He told me about work, and I listened. As far as he knew, no one at the office had addressed his affair with Dharma. According to him, they'd only briefly acknowledged her death. My name would forever be a part of the official police report, but no one ever asked me about it again. The calm after the tragedy was almost as disturbing as the shooting itself.

I worked and kept my distance from Vince, who was the same patient and kind man I'd fallen in love with. I couldn't imagine a time when I would deserve him, but I knew it wasn't now. Dharma's death remained on my conscience, and I couldn't find a way to put her in the past. I needed some clarity.

I drove James home from soccer while both of us watched the fields pass by in silence. I needed to ask about his day. How he was doing in math? If he liked the book they were reading in class, and if he had fun at recess. I couldn't bring myself to start the conversation, though. I was failing my children, and I couldn't figure out how to stop or how to turn things around.

I mindlessly brought the Escalade to a stop at the corner near our house.

"You know we're still moving," James said. His words broke through the criticism in my head.

"What?"

"We're still moving," he repeated confidently. "Even when we stop, the universe is still expanding at forty-two miles per second." I stared at my gifted son, and the tiniest smile appeared on his face. "No matter what we do. We keep moving."

I nodded at him. "I agree." I turned on my blinker and drove home.

BRAD CAME HOME EARLY FROM work to the house I'd made him buy. He didn't hate it the way he used to. He didn't hate anything the way he used to. "Meredith," he yelled as he knocked on the back door. I leaned away from the counter and saw he was carrying a large plant. I dried my hands on a dishtowel and ran to open the door. He stepped inside and handed me a rubber tree plant.

Brad smiled and sang, "He's got high hopes." He kissed my stunned cheek.

"Thanks," I said and carried the plant to the island.

"You know, when I was in London last week, I did a lot of thinking."

"Wow," I said. My words to Brad were always dripping with sarcasm or despise. I think he preferred the sarcasm.

"You've got to get over this whole thing."

I turned to him, utter hatred filling every corner of my body. The sight of him made me sick. "How can you get over it so quickly? Don't you have a heart?"

"I do, and it never belonged to Dharma. It's sad. I feel bad about it, but I wasn't in love with her, and I'm grateful it was her instead of you." He was disgusting.

"Don't you feel any responsibility? After all, you were sleeping with her for more than two years, right?" I returned to chopping the peppers in front of me.

"Is that what's going on with you? You blame yourself for Dharma's death?" Brad grabbed my wrist. He took the knife from my hand and placed it on the counter. "Dharma was crazy." I winced and shook my head. "I know it's not a nice thing to say, but there was something wrong with her. I tried to cut things off with her for months, and she did everything in her power to keep me. She was completely unreasonable and always unpredictable. She didn't care who she hurt, including you and our children. I'm not happy she's dead, but I'm thrilled she's out of my life."

"You're a bastard."

"I never said I wasn't."

I turned my body and mind away from him, shutting him out and letting him know I wasn't speaking to him anymore. I finished cooking dinner, and we all ate like a real family, one not marred by lies and infidelity. I stared out the window at the rolling field behind our property. I had my children and the most wonderful house in the state, and yet the gaping sinkhole in my chest just kept getting deeper. If I stopped smiling, or stood quiet and alone, I might step into it and disappear into the darkness that was my longing for Vincent Pratt.

"You do realize this is the only planet with windows?" James's question to Liv drug me back to our dinner table.

"You don't know that for sure," Liv debated.

"Yes, I do." He was certain. So sure of himself. He turned to me and asked, "If your brain changes, does that mean your whole personality changes?"

Brad looked at me in wonderment. He still wasn't used to the concepts, equations, and predicaments that interested our children more than toys and winning. I sat back in my chair and basked in the satisfaction that, somehow, I'd managed to protect them from the real world this long. May they never encounter it.

Before I could answer James, he said, "Imagine a hamster with pterodactyl legs and wings."

I shook my head and tried to keep up with his mind. "I—"

"No. Just imagine."

I closed my eyes and dutifully tried to let the image surface. When I opened them, Brad was silently laughing. I smiled at my family and overflowed with love for my children.

When dinner was done, the kids went out back to chase lightning bugs and Brad helped me clean up the dishes. He piled them on the counter by the sink as I rinsed them and put them in the dishwasher. He put the salt and pepper back in the cabinet, wiped off the counter, and pushed all the chairs back in. He was my partner. We were a team.

"I still don't want to lose you," he said, not recognizing I was already gone.

I turned off the faucet and faced my husband. "You never will." We'd be bound together infinitely. "I'll always be the mother of your children."

"But?"

"But we can't stay together."

Brad stood still, watching me and waiting for me to back down. I wasn't the same woman he could talk into things. I wasn't willing to back down on this or anything else where he was concerned. I was done. "And I want sole custody of the kids, since you obviously make poor decisions when it comes to the people you spend your time with. The kids won't ever be around any more of your girlfriends."

"I'm not agreeing to sole custody."

"Yes, you are." Brad stopped moving. He wasn't used to being defied. "Because I remember. Everything. Including you pulling me by the ankle until my skull crashed against the stairs." Brad watched me silently. The confidence drained from his face and left behind the expression of a caught little boy. "I remember how terrified you were that your perfect little family was anything but perfect."

"Were we perfect?" He was back on the offensive. "The whole fight started because you were caught in a lie, or caught in a secret."

"That's ridiculous." I stayed steady. Brad's opinion of me no longer mattered, and neither did the truth of our marriage. "I'm not the kind of woman who has an affair." Brad started to say something and stopped. I lightened and continued. "James and Liv need to wake up here on Christmas morning. You can come stay with us, too. I want our children to love their father. I just need them to see you here, in their house, with me."

"That's crazy." He was indignant.

"I thought you were into crazy."

⁂

I WAITED FOR THE PAPERWORK to be drawn up. Our attorneys went back and forth on a few items, but the only thing I really cared about was the kids. Brad and I each walked away with our inheritance, neither of which amounted to a large sum. He would pay me support for the children and would pay for their college educations. I would take no alimony, but we split the proceeds from the sale of the big house, which, in my mind, had set the whole nightmare into motion.

I kept working at the police station. I increased my hours to full time and put the kids in after-school care. They ended up liking it, and after paying for that and bills, I still had enough money left to save a little. I traded the Escalade for a Honda CR-V and happily drove for days without stopping at the gas station.

"New car?" Vince asked as he held the station door open for me. My arms were loaded with a huge box of police car cupcakes for Daniels's birthday. I'd found the idea on Pinterest and had the bakery make them for me. I was slowly coming around. I thought that was a good thing. Maybe it meant that I was finally *exactly* where I belonged.

"Yes. Things are changing."

"I hope so," he said and took the box from me. He turned

and carried it into the break room, leaving me alone in the lobby, and I realized how faraway I still was from where I truly belonged.

The school year was almost over, and Brad had just closed on his new condo in the city. The kids and I went to visit him there. I tried to keep their lives as normal as possible, and spending a small amount of time with their father was what they were used to. The condo was right across the street from Rittenhouse Square, and we took the kids for lunch outside, where half the tables had dogs lying next to them.

"Can we please get a dog?" Liv asked. "One that will sleep in bed with me."

"It's going to sleep with me," James said, and Liv looked at him as if he were crazy to think a dog—or anything else—would ever choose him over her.

"We'll see," I said, and they both beamed with joy.

Brad raised his eyebrows at me, reminding me it was going to be totally my problem if I got one. I laughed. It had always been only my problem.

But things settled down between us. Brad was an idiot, but he was the only idiot my kids had, and because of that, I wanted him to be happy. He had to be a good dad even if he was a shitty husband. I knew better than anyone that it was possible to separate the two.

When the kids went across the street to run around in the park, Brad asked, "Do you think we should tell them today?"

I watched as James chased Liv around a tree. "I'm in no rush." I regarded my ex-husband. He was older. His young girlfriend had aged him more than she'd saved him. "Unless you think we should tell them."

"Do you not want to tell them because there's some hope we might get back together?"

"No."

"You don't have to answer so fast." Brad laughed a little

"Oh, I do. I think we've officially run our course. But I'm in no rush to change anything about their lives." Liv's laugh could be heard on both sides of the park as James caught her and lifted her off the ground. "They're perfect, you know."

"They ask a lot of fucking questions."

"I know." I could see their smiles from across the street. "They wear me out."

"You're so much better with them than I am."

"You're their father." Dharma flashed through my mind. "Try to keep it that way." Brad reached over to hold my hand, but I pulled it away and placed it back in my lap. I wasn't ready to touch him. "Do you ever think about her?"

Brad ran his hand over the scruff on his chin. "A lot. She haunts me." She'd probably haunt him forever. "And if you knew her, you'd know I mean that literally." Brad picked up the check from the table and read it before placing his credit card in the folder. "How's that awful house of yours?"

"My tavern? Or my church? It's pretty awesome. It's almost completely done."

"We could have waited to sell our house until it was finished."

"I don't mind the construction. Especially since the kids' rooms and the kitchen are done."

"I'm going to rent a house at the shore, and I want you and the kids to come down with me," he said and took another sip of his beer as if we were discussing the weather.

"Vacation together?" I shook my head as I asked the question. He was delusional.

"We can have separate rooms. Unless you insist on sleeping with me, then maybe I'll let you."

"You don't even like to go to the shore with us. You were bored to tears last year."

"That was before."

"Before what?"

"Before I realized what losing you and the kids felt like. I appreciate every minute with you now."

"I don't think it's a good idea." I shook my head, dismissing the entire proposal.

"I'll book it, and we can talk about it later."

"Do you hear me when I speak?"

"Of course I hear you. You said you love the shore, and family vacations are important childhood memories."

forty-eight

THE DREAMS STILL CAME EVERY night. I'd seen him almost every weekday for months, and the anticipation of being with him was overcoming the logical argument that I didn't deserve him. After Dharma had died, nothing felt right anymore. Vince was too good to be involved in any part of the Brad-Dharma-Meredith circus. He was too good for me.

But that reality didn't keep the dreams away. It didn't keep me from dropping off papers in his empty office and inhaling deeply just to smell him. It didn't keep me from remembering every inch of his naked body when he spoke to me at work, and it didn't keep me from him. And now that my marriage was done, that couldn't keep me from him, either.

"So how are the renovations going?" he asked. He still always asked me something about my life. Something meaningless to everyone around us, but it was his way of letting me know he still cared about me.

"Actually, they're done. You should stop by after work and see the place." I tried to keep my voice light, but I really just wanted to take him into his office and beg him to touch me.

Vince stood motionless, shocked by the invitation. It could have been just a coworker asking another over to view the recent renovations on their house. Vince still didn't know that Brad didn't live there with me. No one knew but Jenna. He also didn't know my children were staying at my brother's for the weekend.

"I'd love to. Tonight?"

I kept an easy flow to the conversation. "Tonight's fine with us. We'll be there."

"Okay . . ." He waited for more information, but that was all I had to give him. I walked away and wished he'd follow me home right now.

I drove Liv and James to Pennsylvania. I showered. I made a spanakopita, or attempted to make one, and put it in the oven. If Vince still wanted me, we would exist in the light. If he didn't, we'd have a Greek dinner. Either way, I just needed to be with him.

It was the end of June, and the weather was finally warm. I had on a short denim skirt with a sweater. My feet were bare. At almost exactly six o'clock, the doorbell rang. My heart stopped at the sound of the chimes. This was it. There were no more reasons for us to be separated, except the ones that might be lingering in Vince's head. He knew everything. But I wouldn't give him up without him forcing me to. He was at the door to my house, and it felt more right than anyone who'd ever come before him.

I opened the door, and he was still in his uniform. The one that made my heart skip every single time I saw him in it. I took a few extra seconds to appreciate him, mainly his shoulders and chest before landing on his beautiful green eyes and taking my time there, too. A warmth spread through me. I could have melted.

"Meredith?" he said, a smile covering the entire bottom half of his face.

"Hi." I stepped back and held the door open. "Come in."

Vince stepped past me, and I lowered my head, inhaling him and praying he still wanted me the way I needed him. His presence in my house was a drug. His closeness sent me back to his cabin in my mind, solidifying the fact that I was done living without him. If he didn't want me after everything we'd been through, I would settle for a friendship. That was worth more than anything.

"Just friends," I muttered, reminding myself I already had more from him than I deserved.

"Hmm?"

"Nothing. Did you come right from work?"

"Sorry." Vince looked down at his uniform and then back at me. He knew how his uniform affected me.

"I'll bet." I turned and walked toward the great room. "I'll show you around." I could feel him following me, and instead of a nice dinner, I considered abandoning the plan and attacking him on my couch. My eyes wandered to the countertop in the far room.

Maybe in the kitchen . . .

"Was this the original bar?" Vince dragged my mind back to the house.

"It was." I loved having him in my space. Sharing this with him. "The house has an extraordinary story." He walked around and perused the walls, the windows and their sills, and the hearth. "Speaking of bars, would you like a drink?"

Vince relaxed right in front of me. He looked around the rest of the house that was visible and listened to the silence, and then he looked at me. "I'll have what you're having."

I paused, unable to release him from my sight long enough to pour him a glass of wine. I slowly walked to the kitchen with Vince following me.

"When you said 'we,' I was expecting your family to be here. At least the kids."

"No," I said and poured his wine. I took a sip of my own, still cherishing the sight of him. "I meant me and the fish." I nodded toward the two fish tanks on the counter. "The one on the left belongs to James. His name is Bolt because he's fast. The one on the right is Michael. Liv used an old baby name book to name him."

"Where is everyone?" Vince took his first sip of wine. "And is that spanakopita?" He laughed aloud as he walked over to examine my concoction closer.

"I think it is. I tried." I walked up behind him and buried my face between his shoulder blades. My body relaxed at the touch of him. He was my safety. I inhaled deeply as I wrapped my arms around him and laid my hands flat on his stomach. He was strong and solid. I closed my eyes as peace overcame me.

"I don't know what's going on," he said. His voice was low.

"I know."

He turned around and ran his hands through my hair. He tilted my head up to his and kissed me, and every single wrong in the world was righted by his tongue in my mouth. He would fuel the good inside me, and I'd be better because he was near me. He pulled away from my lips and rested his forehead against mine.

"What is going on?"

"It's a date. It's our first date. If you want it to be."

His body stayed perfectly still in my arms. The seconds dragged by as his eyes searched mine for answers.

Vince took a step back from me. I couldn't tell what he was thinking or if there was still hope for me. "What's changed?"

"Everything. Except the way I love you."

"I still don't understand." His voice was low, his words were even. Vince would not falter.

"I'm no longer married. The kids and I live here alone." He lowered his head, and I watched his chest rise as he inhaled. His silence was my tribulation. Why wasn't he saying anything? Why didn't he tell me he loved me? First, I found my breath, and then I found my voice. It was unsteady as I said, "If you'll still have me. I'm saying the word."

He looked up at me. He was trapped some place between desire and rage. For the first time, I had no idea what Vince was thinking. "Which one?"

I pressed myself against him. I stood on my tiptoes and kissed him on the cheek. "All of them."

"Meredith." He was on top of me. Pressing me back against the island as he said, "This is the truth?"

"Always." He kissed me, and I was lost in Colonel Vincent Pratt. "It's real. We're real."

"We're here all alone?" he asked, breathless, in my ear.

"All alone. All weekend."

His lips trailed down my neck. "That's some first date."

"I know. Are you free for the next forty hours?" I reached down and stroked him through his uniform pants.

"I'm free for the next forty years."

Please see the next page for an excerpt of the stunning first installment of The Lost Souls Series.

Forgive Me
Available now.

Forgive Me

~ 1 ~

"My soul is forgotten, veiled by a boring complication"

MY FOOT WILL BLEED SOON. Judging by the familiar curve in the road, I'm still at least two miles from home. Of course I end up walking home the night I'm wearing great shoes. The pain shoots through my heel as the clouds flash with lightning in the dark sky.

Maybe I'm bleeding already. I mentally review the last few hours. Anything to distract me from the agony of each step. The texts, the endless stream of drunken texts, run through my mind.

We're soul mates. I roll my eyes. Brian deserves a nicer girlfriend; someone sweet like him. Someone who doesn't roll their eyes at this statement.

We belong together. Bleh.

What does it say about my relationship when the only thing I ever tell people about my boyfriend is, "He's a really nice guy"? And how, after two years of being apart, did I ever take him back? The last three weeks have felt like years, years I was asleep.

We're perfect together. My mother thought we were perfect. Hell, this whole town thought it.

No one is ever going to know you the way I do. He was watching me as I read this one and I had to work hard to keep a straight face. At the time I wasn't sure why, but here on this deserted road, in the middle of a thunderstorm Brian would never walk through, I know it's because he never knew me at all. Or my soul. It's not his fault. I'd nearly forgotten it myself.

I stop to adjust the strap on my sandals and two sets of eyes peer out from the ditch next to the road. They're low to the ground, watching me. I've always hated nocturnal animals.

"Anyone else come out to play in the storm?" I say to the other hidden night life. I move to the edge of the shoulder, facing the nonexistent traffic, and give my new friends some room. I wince as I step forward, and watch as a set of headlights shines on the road in front of me and the scene around me turns mystical. The steam rises off the pavement at least five feet high before disappearing into the blue tinted night. The rain only lasted twenty spectacular minutes, not long enough to cool the scorched earth.

I'm lost in it as the truck pulls up beside me, now driving on the wrong side of the road, and Jason Leer rolls down his window. I glance at him and turn to stare straight ahead, trying not to let the excruciating torture of each step show on my face.

"Hi, Annie," he says, and immediately pisses me off. I might look sweet in my new rose-colored shorts romper, but these wedges have me ready to commit murder.

"My name is Charlotte," I say without looking at him, and keep walking. The strap is an ax cutting my heel from my foot. *Why won't he call me Charlotte?* Of course the cowboy would show up. What this night needs is a steer wrestler to confound me further. The same two desires he always evokes in me surface now. Wanting to punch him, and wanting to climb on top of him.

"What the hell are you doing out here? Alone—" A guttural moan of thunder interrupts him, and I tilt my head to determine the origin, but it surrounds us. The clouds circle, blanketing us with darkness, but when the moon is visible it's bright enough to see in this blue-gray night. We're in the eye of the storm and there will never be a night like this again. *God I love a storm.* The crackling of the truck's tires on the road reminds me of my cohort.

"I'm not alone. You're here, irritating me as usual." I will not look at him. I can feel his smartass grin without even seeing him, the same way I can feel a chill slip across my skin. It's hot as hell out and Jason Leer is giving me the chills.

Lightning strikes, reaching the ground in the field just to our left, and I stop walking to watch it. Every minute of today brought me here. The mind-numbing dinner date with Brian Matlin, the conversation on the way to Michelle's party about how we should see other people, the repeated and *annoying* texts declaring his love, and the eleven beers and four shots I watched Brian pour down his throat, all brought me here.

"If you're trying to kill yourself by being struck by lightning, I could just hit you with my truck. It'll be faster," he says, stealing my eyes from the field. His arm rests out his truck window and it's enormous. He tilts his body toward the door and the width of his chest holds my gaze for a moment too long.

"Annie!"

I shake my head, freeing myself from him. "What? What do you want? I'm not afraid of a storm." I am, however, exhausted by this conversation.

I finally allow myself to look him in the eyes. They are dark tonight, like the slick, steamy road before me, and I shouldn't have looked.

"I want you." His voice is tranquil, as if he's talking the suicide jumper off the bridge. "I want you to get in the truck and

I'll drive you home." Thunder growls in the distance and the lightning strikes to the left and right of the road at the same time. The storm surrounds us, but the rain was gone too soon. Leaving us with the suffocating heat that set the road on fire.

I close my eyes as my sandal cuts deeper into my foot, and Jason finally pulls away. My grandmother always said the heat brings out the crazy in people. It was ninety-seven degrees at 7 P.M. The humidity was unbearable. Too hot to eat. Too hot to laugh. The only thing you could do was talk about how miserably hot it was outside. By the time Brian and I arrived, most of the party had already been in the lake at some point. Even that didn't look refreshing. The sky unleashed, and Michelle kicked everyone out rather than let them destroy her house.

I stop walking, and shift my foot in the shoe. The strap is now sticking; I've probably already shed blood. Jason drives onto the right side of the road and stops the truck on the tiny shoulder. He turns on his hazard lights and gets out of the truck. *He's a hazard.* I plaster a smile on my face and begin walking again. As soon as he leaves I'm taking off these shoes and throwing them in the pepper field next to me.

Before I endure two steps, he's in front of me. He's as fast as I remember. Like lightning: always picked first for kickball in elementary school. His hair is the same thick, jet black as back then, too. The moonlight shines off it and I wonder where his cowboy hat is. He's too beautiful to piss me off as much as he does. He blocks my path, a concrete wall, and I stop just inches from him.

"I'm going to ask you one more time to get in the truck." A lightning strike hits the road near his truck and without flinching he looks back at me, waiting for my answer.

"Or what?" I challenge him with my words and my "I dare you" look on my face. He hoists me over his shoulder and walks back to the truck as if I'm a sweatshirt he grabbed as an afterthought before walking out the door.

"Put me down! I'm not some steer you can toss around," I yell, as I fist my hands and pound on his back. He's laughing and pissing me off even more. I pull his shirt up and start to reach for his underwear and Jason runs the last few steps to the truck.

"Do you ever behave?" he asks, and swings the truck door open. He drops me on the seat and leans in the truck between my legs. I push my hair out of my face, my chest still heaving with anger. "Why the hell are you walking alone on a country road, in a goddamned storm, this late at night?"

My stomach knots at his closeness and this angers me, too. Why can't Jason Leer bore me the way Brian Matlin does? Jason raises his eyebrows and tilts his head at the perfect angle to send a chill down my spine.

"Brian and I broke up tonight."

"And he made you walk home?" Shock is written all over his face. Brian would never make me walk home. He is the nicest of guys. Not great at holding his liquor, but nice.

"No." I roll my eyes, calling him an idiot, and he somehow leans in closer, making my stomach flip. "He proceeded to get drunk at Michelle Farrell's party and I drove him home so he didn't die." I think back to all the parties of the last six years, since Jason and I entered high school. Besides graduation, we were rarely in the same place. I've barely hung out with Jason Leer since eighth grade. At the start of high school everyone broke into groups, and this cowboy wasn't in mine.

"Why didn't you call someone for a ride?" He breaks my revelry.

"Because apparently when Brian gets drunk he texts a lot. My battery died after the fiftieth message professing his love for me."

"Poor guy."

"Poor guy? What about me? I'm the one who had to delete them, and drive him home. I thought he'd never pass out." I'm still mourning the time I lost with Brian's drunken mess.

"Why didn't you just take his car?"

"Because I left him passed out in it in his parents' driveway. I got him home safe, but I'm not going to carry him to bed."

At this Jason lowers his head and laughs. My irritation with him twists into annoyance at myself for telling him anything. For telling him everything. I want to punch him in his laughing mouth. His lips are perfect, though.

"It's not easy to love you, Annie."

"Yeah, well I've got fifty texts that claim otherwise. Judging from the fact you can't even get my name right, everything's probably hard for you." Jason leans on the dash and his jeans scrape against my maimed foot, causing my face to twist in pain. Before I can regain my composure, his eyes are on me. He moves back and holds my foot up near his face. He slips the strap off my heel and runs his thumb across the now broken and purple blister. I close my eyes, the sight of the wound amplifying the pain.

"My God, you are stubborn," he says, his eyes still on my foot. Thunder groans behind us and he straightens my leg, examining it in the glimmer of moonlight. I'm not angry anymore. One urge has silenced another, and awakened me in the process. He pulls my foot to him and kisses the inside of my ankle, and a chill runs from my leg to both breasts and settles in the back of my throat, stealing my breath.

I swallow hard. "Are all your first kisses on the inside of the ankle?" I ask. His hands grip my ankle harshly, but he's careful with my heel.

His eyes find mine as he drags his lips up my calf and kisses the inside of my knee. I shut up and shudder from a chill. There are no words. Only the beginning of a thought. *What if,* arises in my mind against the sound of the clicking of the hazard lights.

The lightning strikes again and unveils the darkness in his

eyes. He lowers my leg and backs up, but I'm not ready to let him go. I grab his belt buckle and pull him toward me. Jason doesn't budge. He is an ox. His eyes bore into me and for a moment I think he hates me. He's holding a raging river behind a dam, and I'm recklessly breeching it.

With a hand gripping each shoulder he forces me back to the seat and hovers over me. Even in the darkness I can see the emptiness in his eyes and I can't leave it alone. He kisses me. He kisses me as if he's done it a hundred times before, and when his lips touch mine some animalistic need growls inside of me. He's like nothing I've ever known, and my body craves a hundred things all at once, every one of them him. With his tongue in my mouth, I tighten my arms around his thick neck and pull him closer, wanting to climb inside of him.

Jason pulls away, devastating me, until I realize there are flashing lights behind us. His eyes fixed on mine, he takes my hands from behind his head and pulls me upright before the state trooper steps out of his car and walks to our side of the truck.

❧

"CHARLOTTE, HONEY, ARE YOU GOING to get up? I heard you come in late last night."

I roll over and put my head under the pillow. I don't want to get up. I don't want to tell my mom that I broke up with Brian . . . again.

"Is everything okay?" She's worried. I take a deep breath and sit up in bed. The sheet rubs against my heel and the pain reminds me of Jason Leer.

"I broke up with Brian last night."

"Oh no. I have to see his mother at Book Club on Wednesday."

"I can't marry him because you can't face his mother at Book Club."

"I'm not suggesting you marry him, just that you stop dating him if you're going to keep breaking his heart." My mom leaves my room. Her face is plagued with frustration mixed with disappointment. I climb out of bed and lumber to the bathroom. My green eyes sparkle in the mirror, hinting at our indelicate secret from last night. I wink at myself as if something exciting is about to happen. My long blond hair barely looks slept on. I think breaking up with Brian was good for me.

"Jack, she broke up with Brian again." I catch, as I enter the kitchen.

"Through with him, huh?" My father never seems to have an opinion on who I date as long as they treat me well. Brian certainly did that.

"Dad, he just didn't do it for me." Jason's eyes pierce my thoughts again, haunting me. The trooper sent us home and I left him in his truck without a word. There wasn't one to say.

"Do what? What did you expect him to do for you?" my mother spouts. She's not taking the news well.

"When he looks at me a certain way, I want to get chills," I start, surprised by how easily my needs are verbalized. "When he leans into me, I want my stomach to flip, and when he walks away I want to care if he comes back." My parents both watch me silently as if I'm reciting a poem at the second-grade music program. They are pondering me.

"What? Don't your stomachs flip when you're together? Ever?"

"Does your stomach flip when you look at me, Jack?" she asks.

"Only if I eat chili the same day," my dad says, and they both start laughing.

"Charlotte, I remember what it was like to be young. And your father did make my stomach flip, but I think you're too hard on Brian. He's a nice boy."

"Yeah yeah. He's nice." I butter my toast and move to sit next to my father at the table. *He is nice.* For some reason Brian's kindness frustrates me. He's a boring complication. "I ran into Jason Leer last night." *And he kissed the inside of my leg.* I smile ruefully.

My mother's eyebrows raise and I fear I've divulged too much. My father never looks up from the newspaper.

"Butch and Joanie's son?"

"That's the one." I try to sound nonchalant as a tiny chill runs down my neck.

"I haven't seen him since Joanie's funeral. Poor boy. She was lovely. Do you remember her?"

I nod my head and take a bite of the toast. "From Sunday school."

"Jack, do you remember Joanie Leer? Died of cancer about a year ago."

"I remember," my dad says, and appears to be ignoring us, but I know he's not. He always hears everything.

"If you don't want to be with Brian, that's fine, but please not a rodeo cowboy," my mother pleads, not missing a thing.

"I only said I saw him. What's wrong with a rodeo cowboy?"

"Nothing. For someone else's daughter. I really want you to marry someone with a job. Someone that can take care of you."

"Can't a cowboy do that?" *From what I've seen, he can take very good care of me.*

"Charlotte, please tell me you're not serious. They're always on the road. Their income's not steady. It's a very difficult life." My mother's stern warning is delivered while she fills the dishwasher, as if we're discussing a fairytale, a situation so absurd it barely warrants a discussion. She's still beautiful, even when she's lecturing me. "I know safe choices aren't attractive to the young, but believe me you do not belong in that world and he'd wither up and die in yours. Do not underestimate the power of safety in this crazy life."

"How do you know so much about rodeo cowboys?" I ask.

"Yeah, how do you know so much?" My dad asks. He stares at her over the newspaper.

"Is your stomach flipping?" She asks, and gives him her beautiful smile she's flashed to quell him my entire life.

"Yes," he says, and winks at her.

Forgive Me
Available Now

about the author

ELIZA FREED GRADUATED FROM RUTGERS University and returned to her hometown in rural South Jersey. Her mother encouraged her to take some time and find herself. After three months of searching, she began to bounce checks, her neighbors began to talk, and her mother told her to find a job.

She settled into corporate America, learning systems and practices and the bureaucracy that slows them. Eliza quickly discovered her creativity and gift for story telling as a corporate trainer and spent years perfecting her presentation skills and studying diversity. It was during this time she became an avid observer of the characters she met and the heartaches they endured. Her years of study taught her that laughter, even the completely inappropriate kind, was the key to survival.

She currently lives in New Jersey with her family and a misbehaving beagle named Odin. As an avid swimmer, if Eliza is not with her family and friends, she'd rather be underwater. While she enjoys many genres, she is, and always has been, a sucker for a love story . . . the more screwed up the better.

To keep up with all of Eliza's new releases and giveaways, sign up for her newsletter at *www.elizafreed.com/love-letters.html*.

www.ingramcontent.com/pod-product-compliance
Lightning Source LLC
Chambersburg PA
CBHW071252250626

47159CB00004B/1146